THE
SCENT
OF
POPPIES

THE SCENT OF POPPIES

Rex Collings

A Deirdre McDonald Book
London

First published in 1994
by Deirdre McDonald Books
128 Lower Richmond Road
London SW15 1LN

Copyright © Rex Collings 1994

The right of Rex Collings to be identified as
the author of this Work has been asserted by him
in accordance with the Copyright, Designs & Patents
Act 1988

All rights reserved

All the characters in this book
are fictitious and any resemblance
to actual persons, living or dead,
is purely coincidental

ISBN 1 898094 03 9

Designed by Mick Keates
Phototypeset by Intype, London
Printed and bound in Great Britain
by Hartnolls Ltd

Prologue

'A time to kill, and a time to heal; a time to mourn
and a time to dance'

On a still day the waters of Loch Awe, in that stretch below the pumping station, are as black and translucent as obsidian; however strongly one strains to pierce the depths all that one can see is the reflection of the bare sides of the mountains or, if one is close, the shadow of one's own countenance. It is a huge natural looking-glass protecting, concealing what lies beneath it.

One late spring day before the tourists, holiday makers and travellers had set up their tents, peace and a pleasant emptiness characterized the Highlands. A man stood by his car smoking a thin black cigar, gazing down at the waters. He was a small man of less than average height, nondescript, unnoticeable in a crowded room or a busy railway station, very quick on his feet and neat in his movements. He was a most effective operative, especially as he could disappear in four languages. His colleagues in the department knew little of his private, unofficial life; his superiors consulted his personal file from time to time and updated it. This day it would have shown them that he was thirty-six, married to a primary school teacher, with a daughter of thirteen; that he lived in Kenton in a semi-detached three bedroom two-storeyed house built in the thirties, that he kept his garden neat, that the lawn was mown regularly and the privet hedge clipped. He had neither a mistress nor a drink problem. He was wholly unmemorable. An hour later he was dead.

A broken neck, so said the doctor who had inspected the body. There would certainly have to be an inquest. The local policeman found it difficult to understand how the car had gone over the edge into the loch below. It was a mystery. It took three men to bring the body to the ambulance. The only identification was an American Express card, an MCC membership card and a business card with a company's address and a London telephone number. When the policeman telephoned the number and explained why he was ringing he was amazed at the response. Within minutes, or so it seemed to him, a top man from Glasgow had taken over. A helicopter arrived bearing not gods but a plain-clothes, grim-faced man, his secretary and a photographer.

'We will take over,' the constable was told. They did, completely.

CHAPTER ONE

Tributaries

'Any man's death diminishes me, because I am involved in Mankind'

It is difficult to know where to begin; stories, like many rivers, generally have a multitude of sources. The Thames is fed by dozens of tributaries; thus if one were so foolish or so ill-advised, even today, to drink a tumbler of water taken from below London Bridge its contents might well have come, in part at least, from one of those little streams that flow through the quiet untroubled water meadows above Abingdon, meadows where in my grandmother's early Victorian girlhood fritillaries flowered in profusion, and not from the spring at the source nor indeed from the sewers of the Middlesex and Surrey suburbs. Years ago when I worked in Africa I used often to stand on the banks overlooking the Ripon Falls in Uganda at the place where the Nile leaves Victoria Nyanza; although there is now no longer a Falls to see, for the hydro-electric dam further down the river has drowned them. I have stood there on the banks and watched the water flow by, water that perhaps days later would flow as thick and dense as Brown Windsor Soup beneath the Cairo bridge which I would cross walking from the hotel to the Gezira Club.

Where shall I begin?

It was some years after the war, the Second World War, had ended, although National Service was still obligatory. I had lately finished my service in the Army – this had included a stint in Korea – and was sailing to Kenya in one of the steamers of the old British India Line to visit my father who, since his early retirement and the sale of the family business, had settled in Molo, breeding sheep. Molo lamb in those days was quite famous. I was travelling in some style, first class, a gift from my father. 'Once at least', he had written, 'you should travel comfortably, you have endured enough discomfort in Korea.' Korea, the Korean War, today, seems generations ago. It was when on leave in Tokyo from the frozen Korean front – not at all like the sanitized, civilized, zany world of M.A.S.H. – it was then during a drunken, dimly remembered, mindless celebration that I lost my virginity: a disastrous occasion better forgotten but indelibly imprinted on my mind. 'And', the letter from my father had said, 'when you book your ticket insist on a cabin on the port side on the way out and on the starboard side on the way back. It is, you know, the origin of "posh": Port Out, Starboard Home? You will escape the blazing sun of the Red Sea in this way.'

I had taken his advice; my cabin was next to that of a young doctor, not long qualified, on his way to Southern Rhodesia. He was, he told me, half French half Scottish – his name Paul Gustave Murdo MacLean, Gustave after his French great-grandfather. We became friends, one of those sudden, close, intense shipboard friendships without barriers that so often blossom and which so soon die once land is reached; but our friendship did not die, it flowered and for a time I used to see him quite often. He drove from Rhodesia to Kenya on local leave when I was there and returned to London after his first short tour of duty in Salisbury ended, soon after I did. We saw a good deal of each other in London until he married, then he 'got' religion rather badly and returned to Central Africa as a medical missionary. He joined the Protestant sect of which his wife, Elizabeth, was a devoted, almost fanatical member.

I stayed in Nairobi for over a year, rather longer than I had planned. Shortly after I landed I had met a young actress, Hélène, at the Donovan Maule theatre and fell, or so I believed at the time, hopelessly in love. Although I asked, she refused to marry me but we lived together, spasmodically and not very successfully, for some months. This affair ended suddenly and tragically when her Volkswagen overturned at one of the rail crossings on the Nakuru road, which was notorious for its dangerous bends. Most dear Hélène; I loved her, but we were ill-matched. In those months together there were moments of great tranquillity but, alas, too often we fought or bickered or sulked.

Hélène was breathtakingly beautiful, with a rich husky voice and a faint French accent – which on stage she could, if necessary, shed without effort. She was like a malachite kingfisher which hangs in the air, a rainbow jewel, before hurtling and disappearing into the water beneath. A jewel, a lovely lonely jewel, so elusive that when I stretched out my hand to grasp it, it would dissolve, vanish. She had come to Kenya because the job was attractive and she wanted to escape for a time from the cold and dampness and restrictions of England and from the interminable grind of provincial tours. In Nairobi as one of the most beautiful women as well as the most talented actress she was free of competition, she held court – 'the stars her courtiers yet'.

When there was an evening performance at the theatre, if not already there, I would drive into Nairobi and fetch her, and bring her back to the rondaval in Limuru where I was staying. Once in the car she would begin complaining, bitching, unhappy with the audience's response to the performance, or with her colleagues; she would turn on me and I would be goaded into shouting at her – and the journey would end in silence. She never drank, perhaps alcohol would have helped her to unwind. Most evenings, after a scratch meal, she would take two strong sleeping tablets before being able to find sleep. On these nights too she would turn from my touch with a bitter remark, and I would lie watching her, helpless, silent and frustrated, unable to connect. But on other days when she was between plays, or on one of those rare occasions when her understudy was to be given an opportunity to show her paces, we would sit after supper on the little verandah. With the lights switched off because of the insects, I would lie in one of those wicker chairs with an extension for one's legs and she would sit on the stool end by my feet. Often she would fetch her guitar and sing to me the soft sad songs of her childhood, and Scottish and English laments, in her beautiful husky voice, a voice that caressed and soothed and in the end excited. In the background all the noises of Africa, in the heavens a clear sky; the moon when full touched her with ethereal magic. She would sing those songs of my choosing; even today to hear one of them is to bring back her presence, even her warm and lovely human smell. These were the golden times; when we went in, our bodies followed our minds without impediment.

> They told me lies
> They said:
> You will forget
> Love dies.

Soon after her death I came home; it was shortly after this that Paul's contract in Rhodesia had ended and he too had returned to Britain. When Paul later married, his wife did her uttermost to break our friendship. She was, or so I thought, a shrew, blinkered and mean. She could not conceal her disapproval of me and of my style of living, and she distrusted a relationship in which there was no place for her. Elizabeth persuaded Paul to return to Rhodesia as a medical missionary and this meant that for over twelve years we had not met, although we had written to each other at regular intervals and his son Gordon Rory was my godson, by proxy. I knew him, Rory that is, only from the photographs that came regularly at Christmas. There was one other child, a daughter, Penelope, older than Rory.

This is the beginning, at least part of it, part of the background. After I had returned to London, unhappy and disillusioned, after Hélène's death, I had prospered, first working as an editor in a large publishing house, then with some of the money that had been left me by my mother buying a partnership in a smaller, more specialised firm. Today, I write biographies of the great travellers and explorers part of the time and edit and publish the rest of the time. I have a flat in London, in Marylebone, and a cottage in the Highlands, a substantial stone cottage to which I have added a library-cum-study; one side being mostly glass, double-glazed, with a marvellous view across the loch. A beautiful, magic place, nun-like, so peaceful and remote. Otters come to the shore and seals lie basking on the rocks at low tide in front of the cottage; Sika deer in the early morning look over the gate lusting after my vegetables. It was a haven of great peace. In the village nearby lived my old Nanny, which was the reason why I had come to the place in the first instance. Nanny McPhee lived with her sister, the local postmistress. Nanny kept an eye on me. She sewed and mended, scolded and reproved; and she bullied the woman who, when I was there, came in to scrub and clean.

It was a good arrangement for me, it meant that all I had to do was to telephone from London and say, 'Nanny I'll be up tomorrow,' and I knew that the bed would be made and aired, food and milk got in, and in winter a fire lit. A somewhat pampered but wholly delightful existence – I was very fortunate. The only fly in this ointment was her vocal disapproval of a number of my friends. Nanny had strong opinions which, although I often angrily rejected them, were usually and depressingly proved in the long run to have been well founded.

My work as a sponsoring editor involved me in a certain amount of travelling overseas and I was, in early July, in Johannesburg, the dry winter season when it could sometimes be cold enough even for snow. I came back to my hotel at lunchtime to dump some scripts and papers; there was a message waiting for me from London – would I please ring as a matter of great urgency Mr Jones on a London number on an important personal matter. This I did – it turned out to be the number of the headquarters of Paul's Mission. I learned to my horror that terrorists – it was a short time before the Lancaster House accord – had raided the Mission Station and butchered, indiscriminately, the white and black staff. Elizabeth and Penelope were both dead, but when the defence forces had arrived Paul was still alive, but only just; he was dying and was asking for me. Rory, boarding at a prep school in Salisbury, was safe.

'Could you please', I was asked, 'fly to Rhodesia and go to the hospital?' The Mission was prepared if necessary to foot the bill.

I could and I did; next day I was by Paul's bed. 'I'm dying,' he said. 'I know I am, so don't pretend, don't make a fuss, please.' Then after a silence, 'I want you to become Rory's guardian, take my place. I don't want those awful cousins of Elizabeth to get their claws into him, they're maniacs. Please, Adam, please?' I had no choice. Who can deny or argue with a dying friend? The lawyer was called and the papers that he had already prepared were signed and witnessed and the doctor's deposition taken. It was settled: in the event of Paul's death I was to be Rory's guardian.

Paul had been flown by army helicopter to Salisbury and Rory visited the hospital each day, but he had not been told, explicitly, the seriousness of his father's condition. We met briefly after the papers had been signed. Paul then said: 'Rory, this is Uncle Adam, my dearest friend, trust him always. I do.'

I stayed by Paul's bed, he held my hand most of the time. Two days later he was dead. I wept; for our lost opportunities, for his great beauty, for my love, for the senseless waste. 'Jonathan', I thought, 'my brother Jonathan very pleasant hast thou been unto me, thy love to me was wonderful.' After the funeral I went to the school to collect

Rory. The headmaster had thought, and I had agreed with him, that it was better that he should not have been at the service. There were no family possessions to be collected, fire had destroyed everything at the Station. All there was left was one male six-year-old child, almost a complete stranger, with a shabby leather suitcase and an airbag full to bursting: and I was his legal guardian. I took him to the house of a school friend where he spent his last days in Salisbury. It was only after a couple of days of intensive, frenetic action that it was possible, legally, for me to take Rory from the country; fortunately he had been born in England and his passport was British – for some reason that I never discovered he had not been put on either of his parents', probably because he had travelled once on his own to South Africa.

In the latter days of UDI there were no direct flights to Britain; we had to go through Johannesburg. Rory, not surprisingly, was silent and still, showing little emotion and no interest in the flight. He understood from what his father had said, and what his headmaster had explained after the funeral, that I would now be his guardian, that I would be his 'family'. A great deal for a small boy, confused and battered by the recent events, to accept – only a week ago he had been part of a real family, secure in their love and care; now he was alone.

I had some business to conclude in Johannesburg and in any case I had been unable to book seats on a plane home for some days. This meant spending three nights there. I had booked a room in the Carlton, and we drove there in a taxi from Jan Smuts airport. I had tried to talk to Rory on the plane but it was difficult to maintain a reasonable conversation with someone who answered politely enough but in monosyllables and who showed little interest in the places or people around him. I had decided that a double room was the better (as well as the cheaper) choice: a lonely little boy on the twentieth floor of a strange hotel, out of my watchful eye, did not seem a good idea.

'Rory,' I said when unpacking had been finished, 'I think if you don't mind we'll go down to the Coffee Shop now, and you can have your supper – I'll eat later, one of my business friends is coming here to see me; but he and I will eat here in the hotel, we won't go out, is that OK?'

'Yes,' he answered. We went down to the Coffee Shop where he ate seriously but unenthusiastically an omelette and chips and drank a glass of whiter than white milk. I had a cup of coffee. We then went back to our room.

'Look, old chap,' I said, 'you have your bath and then go to bed, you've got something to read haven't you?'

'Yes, thank you.'

'Do you want any help, can you manage?'

'I'm all right, thank you.'

He bathed, I heard him splashing a little, not for very long, then clad in pyjamas he stood before me, hair plastered down, a glowing steaming shrimp of infinite sadness.

'Have you cleaned your teeth?'

'Yes, Uncle.'

'Good.'

The telephone rang, I answered it. My guest had arrived. I bent and kissed Rory's forehead. 'Good night, old chap. Remember, I'll be in the hotel all the time, I am not going out. If you want me, all you have to do is to dial Reception – look, here's the number – 2 – and ask them to page me. Tell them I'm probably in one of the restaurants or bars – is that all right?'

'Yes,' he answered.

'Are you sure?'

'Yes, thank you.'

The rest of the evening passed quickly enough. Lionel and I concluded our business and spent a profitable and companionable couple of hours talking and drinking. I told Lionel about Rory.

'You've certainly got yourself a problem,' he said. 'I don't envy you: you could send him to a boarding school; I suppose there is enough money?'

'Oh yes, Rory is not badly off.' Indeed, with a certain amount of family money and the proceeds of a good insurance policy there was no financial problem to be solved, and I was comfortably off, too.

'But, Lionel,' I said, 'what about the holidays? What about my life? I'm going to be tied, tied for ten years at least.'

'Well, I expect there are holiday camps, and didn't you say that he had some relations, cousins, you could always send him to them, couldn't you?'

'Yes I could but I won't. I promised Paul I would look after Rory, and I'm damned if I'll break that promise. Paul loathed those cousins. Do you know, Lionel, I feel that in the end he hated the Mission. He wanted a different life, not that prayer-bound joyless life that

Elizabeth was so attached to; it was only because he was a doctor and could practise that he stuck it: he really was a healer.'

So we talked, going round and round and finding no solutions. Lionel left after 10.30 and I returned a little glumly to my room. I let myself in as quietly as I could, the lights were out except for the bathroom one, the curtain pulled back to let the moonlight in. Rory appeared to be asleep. I poured myself a whisky and took it into the bathroom. I turned on the taps for a bath, cleaned my teeth and undressed. I looked in the glass and saw dozens of images of myself vanishing into the distance. Oh hell, I thought, looking after this uncommunicative boy is going to take an awful lot of effort. I did not relish the thought of being tied down. After my bath I turned out the light and slipped into bed. I lay still for a few minutes watching the stars high in the sky over the spoil heaps of the old mines – then I became conscious that Rory too was awake, and it sounded as though he were breathing heavily, very probably sobbing.

'Hey,' I said, 'Rory are you all right?'

'Yes,' but it was a stifled, indistinct 'yes'.

I got out of my bed and went over to his, his head was under the sheets, only a tuft of hair showed. I pulled back the sheet, uncovering his head. 'Here, it's all right old chap, I'm here.' I looked down at him for a moment. The little boy turned, looked up at me, and then with one bound was in my arms, sobbing for the first time, clinging to me. I held him tight and carried him back to my bed, his hands locked behind my neck.

'Tonight,' I said, 'just for tonight I think that it might be a good idea if you slept with me, don't you?'

'Yes, oh yes, please.'

Gradually the sobbing ceased and his breathing became more regular. I held him in my arms. He slept; it was not a comfortable night for me. I woke very early, took a bath to ease my stiffness, then ordered some tea. Rory lay curled up, asleep, a peaceful look on his face, a face unclouded by distress. My tea came and I sat by the window, watching the sun rise like an enormous Belisha Beacon behind the spoil heaps.

'Hi, Uncle,' he was beside me, 'can I have tea too?'

What a relief!

'Yes of course you can, just dial Room Service and ask them to send up another tray. Would you like some orange juice? If so, ask for that as well.'

It was a cold, late winter's morning, so I told him to wrap himself in a blanket. He came and stood by my chair and stretched out his hand and touched me. 'It's all right, Uncle,' he said, 'it's all right isn't it?'

'Yes,' I answered, 'it's all right, we'll make do, it'll be a bit tough, but it is all right.'

We flew back to London, and then after sessions with my lawyer to make sure that all was legally correct and that in English law I really was Rory's guardian, we caught a sleeper to Scotland. I had telephoned Nanny and warned her that there was now a new member of the family. At the other end of the line she had clucked away like an old hen, but I knew that by the time we reached the house all would be in order and Rory's room would be ready. Nanny had once met Paul, long ago when he had come here shortly after his marriage. She had liked him but not Elizabeth who had tried to patronize her.

Rory loved the sleeper. He insisted on taking the top bunk, climbing the ladder to go to bed was extremely exciting, so too were the light switches and the air vents.

'Now, go to sleep, there's a good chap, we must get some rest before tomorrow.'

'Aye, aye, Cap'n.' The train had become a pirate's ship. 'Uncle?'

'Yes.'

'I haven't brushed my teeth.'

'All right, you little monster, come and clean them.'

He climbed down.

'I'm not.'

'Not what?'

'I'm not a monster.'

'You are, a horrible monster, you eat time.' I rumpled his hair. 'Good night, monster, now up the ladder, quick, or I'll have the rope's end to you – up.'

'Good night, Cap'n.'

'Night!'

I undressed, got into my bunk, switched off the lights and soon fell asleep. I had decided that at least for the first year or so Rory should not go to a prep school but should go to the village school, in this way we should be able to get to know one another better and establish Rowan Cottage as his home. For companionship I decided to buy a dog. In fact when we went to Oban to look at the Kennels we chose

– or rather Rory fell in love with – a scrap of a West Highland Terrier. We called him Cracker.

Nanny was delighted to have a child to fuss over again and was perfectly happy to move into the house when I had to spend time in London. She had, like most good old-fashioned nannies, no trouble at all in coming to terms with the young. Rory treated her with great respect and affection and was spoiled in return, but it was not the spoiling that results in bad table-manners, tantrums and rudeness.

In the months that followed, Rory and I grew together. I took him on long walks over the hills, showed him where the ravens and eagles nested; and my old friend the minister taught him to fish – an occupation that I abominate. He was happy at the local school and soon made friends with the other children. It was a small school, twenty children in all, the only other boy of his age was Alexander, the son of the doctor, the youngest of a huge family of girls. The practice covered a great spread of the country and the doctor held surgeries in the different villages: but he lived in ours, in a square stone house with a garden that ran down to the river.

Rory made friends easily, two of his closest, and perhaps among the strangest, were the retired Episcopalian priest and his wife who lived in the village. They were former missionaries, he was one of that fast diminishing group of scholars that once had graced the English Church, men regarded as *Stupor Mundi*; she a botanist of professional standing. For old Canon Buchanan and his wife Rory was a surrogate grandchild – their only daughter had died of fever when a child in the days when it was difficult to get drugs in many of the mission stations. Rory spent hours at their house – the Canon was teaching him Latin and Greek and the Canon's wife the violin. From both he learned the names of the flowers and birds and insects; but above all he learnt about bees, the Canon's consuming passion. On the fine long summer evenings when day never seems to die, the Canon would sit in his small orchard among his hives, a book open on his lap, an old stained panama on his head, utterly at peace.

This then is part of the background to the story, to the adventure that followed some years later. A dilettante publisher in early middle age, with a small boy, his ward, living or partly living in a Scottish village, no worries and few problems.

CHAPTER TWO

The Players Take Their Places

'Play up! play up! and play the game!'

THE Long Room was uncomfortably full, the tall stools by the windows all taken; outside the Pavilion the seats, if not actually occupied, were 'booked', cold-bags, coats, newspapers, cushions, squashed hats, indicated that a member had queued early and once in had staked his claim. It was a fine September morning, the first Saturday of the month, the day on which the last one-day cricket final of the season was played. The grass was green, a few patches of damp steamed gently in the morning sun. On this day no guests were allowed in the Pavilion, one's guests, of either sex, if one had had the foresight to apply early in the year for tickets, were welcome in the Warner and Q Stands. There were bars in both.

'If you'll excuse me, old chap, I've got to go to the Warner, I've a guest coming, see you later – love to Fiona.' The speaker, a tallish man in his mid-forties with a florid complexion, a nose showing the first faint signs of purple veins, sporting a blood-and-sand tie of dazzling metallic brightness, extricated himself from a discussion on swing and made his way to the Warner Stand, two cushions dangling from his wrist. He was expensively suited, his hands manicured, his face coarse skinned, pitted with extinct blackheads, but clean as a Turkish bath, he looked what he was, not quite a gentleman – but in a way different from Mr Salteena. He had promised to meet his guest at 9.45. He looked at his watch – gold, quartz and wafer thin. Two minutes to go.

'Ah, Ahmed, punctual as ever.'

'Good morning, Derek, a beautiful day, is it not, for the match?'

'It certainly is. Now, where would you like to sit, up or down?'

'Up, I think.'

'Right.'

The two men climbed the stairs and came out on the balcony. They stood below the commentators' box looking round.

'There, look, there's room for two down there in the first, second, sixth row, let us go there.'

'Excellent.' They edged their way to the seats: put down their papers and score cards. Below them a group of players were practising shots, limbering up; to their right on the small balcony outside one of the changing rooms two white-clad figures were chatting and laughing together. Lord's was filling up rapidly, there was a pleasant bustle, a hum of anticipation.

'Come on, Ahmed, I need a drink.'

The two stood at the bar, the host held a large pink gin, the other, Ahmed, sipped a glass of orange juice.

'Well.'

'Well.'

'Things are not quite as good as they should be, the Scottish connection has been causing trouble.'

'Trouble?'

'Yes, they have attracted unwanted notice. I'm afraid we have had to eliminate part of the opposition, a messy business. For the time being all is quiet but not I think for long, the action taken was too drastic, there are sure to be repercussions.'

'What are you going to do?'

'Close it down, temporarily at least, but that's not really the problem, the problem is that there are reports that a new outbreak of trouble is expected. We have not yet identified the source, but we have sent a couple of good men to keep watch.'

'The other end, Kenya?'

'No problem, that part of the exercise is going well: you've heard nothing have you?'

'No, but I do not trust your man there.'

'Hall: he's all right, a bullshitter I grant you, but perfectly reliable, at least so I've always found and we have a dossier on him that would sink the *Bismarck*. Will you have another one of those?'

'No thank you.'

The other ordered a large pink gin. He held it, took a sip, and turned to his companion.

'Ahmed.'

'Yes, my friend.'

'Are you staying here for long?'

'No, I fly to Karachi on Monday, then later in the month to Nairobi.'

'Good, Eileen should be there then: I shall send her out to make a general survey and report. Does that satisfy you?'

'Yes, excellent. Look, they're going out, we had better get back to our seats.'

'Who won the toss?'

'I don't know. I think we did.'

That day I too was at Lord's, with Rory. I am a member, have been for years, my father had put me down while I was still at my prep school. I was not often in London at the weekends. I tended more and more to go back to Scotland; but cricket was, is, one of my passions and I had taken Rory to the Test to watch the Australians and he had while at school in Salisbury played a little. In the village, school cricket was regarded as a sassanach aberration not to be encouraged. I had made sandwiches and boiled eggs the night before – also mixed the bullshot. Rory had watched me doing this with something akin to awe.

'What are you doing, Uncle?'

'Making bullshot.'

'What's bullshot?'

'Ah, Rory, you're too young, but none the less I'll tell you. It is a drink for hot and cold weather. It is a naval drink and an American drink. I'll show you how it is made, now watch: you take a tin of beef consommé, there, and empty it into this jug, and then another . . . good, now you add the spices.'

'What spices?'

'Oh, anything really that takes your fancy. Look here, we'll put these cloves in, now grate some nutmeg, you grate it but not too much, here's some ginger and cinnamon, a good amount of black pepper and cayenne pepper, now some chopped red chillies.'

'No salt?'

'Yes, put some in, Rory. I think now a generous shaking of Tabasco sauce, stir it up and then heat it. After it has cooled strain and add the vodka. I use one part of vodka to one of consommé, that makes it pretty potent.'

We finished preparing the sandwiches, eggs, and bullshot and put them in the fridge for the next morning.

'Uncle, what'll I drink?'

'Well, what would you like?'

'Coke.'

'Oh dear, I suppose you must, but we'll take some fresh orange juice as well.'

At Lord's on these big days it is my custom to take guests and we sit in the same place each year with a largish group of other habitués. We share a sweepstake, and a certain amount of food and drink, one or two bring children a little older than Rory. My friends are usually an old colleague of my father's from East Africa, a retired government doctor, Richard Dundas, and one of my closest friends, Ned Hoare. Ned knew Rory, for he and his wife had stayed with us a couple of times in Scotland.

The match was between two evenly matched Midland counties. One was my least favourite county, it had too many foreigners in the side and they played undaring cricket – although it was good sometimes to watch the slow bowlers. In the past on our right had been the open space in front of the Tavern Stand bar but for some time now on the big occasions this had been filled with extra seats, a ploy not so much for extra revenue but rather to stop the drunken county supporters making a nuisance of themselves – in a way one missed the authentic rough voice of the committed county supporters – the gentility of 'well played, sir', 'good shot' and 'well taken' can pall after a time.

While we watched I had no idea of the conversation taking place in the Warner Stand, but strangely enough when I went into the Pavilion to spend a penny (the queues outside the general lavatories are unending!) I stopped for a few minutes in the Long Room and stood next to the man who was 'Derek'.

'A good game,' he said. 'I think that last was rather unlucky, it was a brilliant run out.'

'He should have known better than to take chances against this side.'

THE PLAYERS TAKE THEIR PLACES

'Yes, I suppose so.'

Rory took to Dick straight away, and when I got back to my seat they were deep in conversation about spin.

'Uncle, Dick says it is more skilful to be a spin bowler than a fast one, do you think that he is right?'

'I'm not sure, it's arguable, but one thing is certain – a spinner lasts much longer, look at Fred Titmus, he played regularly for Middlesex even after he was forty.'

Lunch came and went in a haze of good food and alcohol – the bullshot had been finished early and we had progressed to wine. Corny old jokes and witticisms seemed exquisitely funny as the day went on: an air of relaxed, undemanding bonhomie engulfed us. The favourites were all out for 242, just over 4 an over. Ned won the sweepstake on the teatime score, Rory had been over-optimistic. After tea the score crept upwards, one batsman made a sparkling 60, another just under 50. But the wickets had fallen too.

The last two overs came: eight wickets had fallen, 21 was needed off twelve balls, the ground was quiet, the bars emptied, there really was a deathly hush. The fast bowler was bowling his last over. Down came his first ball, a scorcher, the batsman touched it and it sped to the boundary, 4 runs, 17 more needed. The second ball was a bouncer, he ducked, no run; the third ball, right in the centre of the bat, a six! The crowd went mad, the fourth ball, pushed to off, they ran one. The tailender, no rabbit, squared up, down came the fifth ball, he never saw it, his off stump leapt into the air, the crowd were in ecstasies. The last man came in, walking slowly, deliberately, through the gloom to the wicket. Calmly he took guard, then the fast bowler, pawing like a bull buffalo about to charge, hurtled down a veritable Exocet of a ball; he never saw it, nor did the wicket keeper, it sped to the boundary for 4 byes, an expensive over – 13 runs scored but a valuable wicket taken. The last over was from a spinner. The batsman took off his helmet, it was no longer needed. Eight runs needed for victory, and only one wicket left to fall. The spinner was a canny bowler, he uses his mind, on his day he can be almost unplayable. Could the batsman risk ones? The first ball beat him but missed the stumps. The second he middled, 4 runs, 4 needed off four balls. The third ball he miss-hit, they ran one – the tension was unbearable, 3 runs off three balls, the tailender had to score, could he? The fourth ball, blocked; the fifth he hit, they ran one, just making it. The scores were equal, one to win. The last ball to come. The batsman, adjusted his box, scratched his ear, surveyed the ground – the fielders on the boundaries were faint figures as dusk fell – down came the last ball with all of the bowler's skill and cunning behind it. The batsman, brilliant, unpredictable, a genius, opened his shoulders, middled it, it hurtled through the air towards the Pavilion, there was a crash of glass – a Long Room window lay shattered. The ground erupted. There was no doubt who would be chosen as the man of the match.

'Whew what a match!'

'What a match.' One of the two elderly men who were sipping whisky in the Members' Bar echoed my exclamation.

'Another one, Jacob?'

'Yes, I think so, thank you.'

He ordered doubles, they drank them without dilution.

'George, I've a problem.'

'Yes.'

'One of my best men was killed a few days ago, his cover was blown, there was a leak, we have found and caulked it.'

' " . . . It is easy to be dead say only this, 'they are dead' then add thereto 'yet many a better one has died before'." '

'Who wrote that?'

'A chap called Sorley, First World War poet – killed on the Front, only twenty or so, he did not write much.'

'Quite good, though, write it down for me sometime, will you?'

'Certainly I will, but what are you going to do?'

'I must have a new face, someone from outside, someone we could trust, my men are known.'

'To do what?'

'To finish what Morgan began, just to tidy up the ends. He would get plenty of support, but he would be on his own for most of the time.'

'How do you find someone like that?'

'By talking to people like you. Do you know anyone? It could be man or woman, but preferably a man in this instance as there is some hard physical work to be done.'

George pondered for a moment or two. Around them men were discussing the match, the excitement of the last two overs and the brilliant last 6 which had broken the window in the Long Room.

'Jacob, you know there may be someone, I've a young chap on

leave from the Gulf, his leave is almost over. I could let him stay if you were interested.'

'What's his name?'

'He's a Scot, a proper Scot born and bred in the Western Highlands, his name is McNab, Michael McNab.'

'McNab, McNab – we would have to check his background – can your office send me all his particulars?'

'Of course, I'll arrange for it to be done on Monday.'

'Um. Do you think he might do?'

'I don't know, a gut feeling, he's a loner, not gregarious, self-contained, at least this is what his records show. Probably homosexual although there is no evidence, but not blatantly so, would that matter?'

'No, it's quite acceptable now so long as it is not hidden, some of our best men are buggers, but then they always were – I'll buy you another, George, then I must go – do you remember that innings of Hammond's in '38 or was it '39?'

The conversation flowed smoothly into the quiet waters of cricket reminiscences, tributaries of the larger river.

CHAPTER THREE

McNab

'Pleasures have mutable faces'

TRIBUTARIES originate in many strange and secret places. Their waters flow into, swell and not infrequently change the course of the main stream as well as its contents. There are two dominant fictional conventions for the siting of the headquarters of the British Secret or Intelligence services. One places it in the back room of a somewhat shabby import-export firm in an unfashionable part of central London where a pipe-smoking headmaster figure with a nicotine-stained moustache sends romantic and usually amateur agents to snatch defeat from the jaws of victory. The other convention places a cold ruthless civil servant in an office somewhere in Whitehall protected by two hundred years of protocol, endless corridors and a discreet secretary, usually a muscular Amazonian figure disguised in large-rimmed spectacles and a swept-back severe hairstyle who, at some stage of the story, will shed the one and unloose the other and appear in a black silk see-through négligé and take the hero unwillingly, exhaustingly and in great detail to bed (this too, occurs in real life if the newspapers and television investigations are to be believed).

The hero, a grammar school boy who has won a scholarship to Oxford (never to a redbrick university) but, through either choice or accident, has failed to acquire the relaxed and phlegmatic approach that in real life is supposedly the product of an Oxbridge education. The Chief, M or C or whatever letter has not been used before will turn out to be a double agent or even a double double agent. This too occurs in real life according to the same newspapers and television investigations.

Michael McNab was a tall, curly-haired Celt born in the Western Highlands, a geologist by training, a loner by instinct and in practice, and under contract for another three years to Consolidated Yemeni Hydro Carbons known on the Stock Exchange as 'Conies'. Michael had received a letter in the penultimate week of his leave asking him to report forthwith to the Brighton Head Office of his company.

The dome of the Pavilion reflected the autumn sunlight, an onion drenched in butter; a breeze from the sea ruffled his hair; he passed a middle-aged woman clutching a plastic carrier bag, a short crimson umbrella, and a lead at the end of which yapped and scuffled one of those irritating miniature poodles, a sorry result of inbreeding. She was muttering to herself and when they passed Michael was able to distinguish what she was saying. 'A third is washing-up liquid: mind that spider, dear, it is a friend.' Everything seemed normal. People unaware of great events were busy staying alive.

Yemeni House, a new glass and steel building, stood at the Kemptown end of the front. Michael had been there before, but he still felt slightly uncomfortable, he did not 'belong'; he automatically smoothed his hair and straightened his tie as he entered the foyer. There was a new receptionist. 'I have an appointment to see Mr George.'

'Your name, sir, please?'

'McNab, Michael McNab.' She turned and spoke into a mouthpiece: 'Jean, Mr McNab's here, he says he has an appointment with Mr George.'

The machine crackled, Michael could not hear what the answer was, but it was obviously affirmatory.

'Yes, sir, Mr George is expecting you, would you take the lift to the top floor. Someone will meet you there.'

'Thank you.'

'You're welcome.'

Michael pressed the button and waited for the lift to come, then he stepped into it and pressed the top button. On the rear wall of the lift was a large looking glass; he looked at himself, straightened his tie again to hide the undone top button of his shirt – service in the tropics had conditioned him to open-necked shirts – and smoothed his eyebrows. The lift arrived with a slight bump, the doors opened and he stepped out on to the thick-carpeted landing lit by a simple glass window that stretched the length of one side, looking out over the sea. A middle-aged woman, substantial in build, neatly not flamboyantly dressed, was waiting for him.

'Mr McNab, good morning.' A rather plummy but not unfriendly voice with a touch of an echo of an accent which he could not quite place.

'Good morning, it's a beautiful view from here.'

'Yes it is, come this way will you, Mr George is expecting you, you're a little late you know.'

'Yes, I'm sorry, but the train got held up outside Hassocks. I think there had been something on the line.'

Jean tutted in sympathy; she was the kind of efficient but maddening secretary who would always tut.

'You're lucky', he continued, 'to work in such a marvellous place. Just look at the sea.'

'Yes, it is nice here, isn't it? Much better than the city: I was so glad we moved.'

She led the way through the outer office and tapped at the inner door. Without waiting for an answer she walked in then stood back for him to pass her.

'Mr McNab, sir.'

Behind the desk was Michael's boss, the wrong end of middle age, above average height; he had a thick thatch of coarse grey hair, a well-trimmed, unstained moustache, shaggy eyebrows reminiscent of those of Denis Healey or the late George Woodcock. He was a man of great drive and ability who had surmounted or, it might be better to say, used his somewhat humble origins to create this large conglomerate of which he was still the head and major shareholder. He wielded with great zest the power that the wealth gave him. He sat with his back to the window; the sunlight blinded Michael.

'Sit down, sit down, like some tea or coffee?'

'Coffee, please, if I may.'

'Good, Jean'll arrange it,' he went on writing, using an old-fashioned fountain pen. It seemed to be made of solid gold. It was that sort of office.

Coffee arrived in a glistening modern pot but with traditional china cups and a plate of gingernuts. Mr George scrawled a signature.

'Jean, take a photocopy of this, then send it by special messenger to Sheikh Abdullah, I want him to have it by late afternoon: use Jimmy if you have to.'

'Certainly, sir.'

Michael wondered whether all this was some form of elaborate play-acting for his benefit.

'Good, had to get rid of that. Well, McNab, enjoying your leave?'

'Yes thank you, sir.'

'Good, I'm glad of that. I want you to extend it, stay here a little longer. Would you mind?'

'No, sir.'

'I expect you are wondering why I asked you down here.'

'Yes, sir, I'm a little mystified.'

'You like scuba-diving,' a statement rather than a question. Michael did not deny it — obviously it was in his file.

'There's a friend of mine who wants to meet you, I'll ask him to come in. Listen to him carefully, he wields a lot of power: help him. You have our full backing.' He pressed a button on the intercom.

'Jean, you there? Good, please ask Sir Jacob to come in if he's ready.'

The door opened and a short, stocky figure came into the room. Mr George stood up. 'Jacob,' he said, 'this is McNab, I think he should be able and willing to help you. McNab, this is Sir Jacob, important government man, Security, don't you know?' Although he had risen from the ranks he had mastered the sentence structures and the style as well as the machine.

Michael took the hand that was offered, the back of it was covered with black matted hair. He thought of chimpanzees.

'Good afternoon, sir.'

'Sit down.' Sir Jacob went behind the desk and sat where Mr George had been sitting, usurping without effort the power and the place: Mr George went out and shut the door quietly behind him.

For a little less than a minute — it seemed much longer as those silences so often do — nothing was said. Sir Jacob was apparently lost in thought. Michael sweated, felt slightly sick and began to think that he wanted to go to the loo.

'Well, McNab, I understand that you may be willing to help us, that'll be most satisfactory. Let me first make something quite clear. We have a file on you, we investigated you very carefully, very carefully indeed, before coming to a decision. Look, this is your file.' When he put it down and opened it Michael saw that its contents included a number of photographs.

Sir Jacob closed the folder and looked straight at Michael.

'You don't much care for women do you?'

Michael felt the blood rise to his face.

'N-no, sir, not very much.'

'There is no need to worry: these things do not matter so much now, so long as we know and you know that we know – eh?'

'Yes, sir.' How much do you know, thought Michael; did they know about his latest affair – the Cypriot draughtsman – Petros, a beautiful young man and most unintelligent. He missed him.

'We checked that young man of yours, Petros, he's clean.'

So they knew. Michael sighed. He had first met Petros after the opening of the new hospital the Company had helped to construct: his boss had come to him and said 'Michael, could you please take young Petros back to town with you, I've got to stay behind with the Minister and we may be some time.' Michael had agreed readily enough and he and Petros had driven back to town in his open Land Rover. When they were near Michael's flat the heavens had opened unexpectedly in one of those extraordinary sudden tropical storms and both had been drenched, water poured off them.

'Come in with me, you can't go on now.' Michael led the way into his flat. 'We had better get out of these clothes: I can lend you some dry ones, OK.' They stripped off. Petros came over to him and put a hand on his bare shoulder and smiled directly at him.

'Thank you, I'm grateful.' After that it was inevitable that they would go to bed together, nakedness, loneliness and lust were irresistible.

It was a pleasant, undemanding relationship. Michael suspected that Petros was simply lonely and accessible and that sooner or later he would settle down and marry. They became friends as well as lovers, played tennis and chess together. Often Petros cooked for Michael. Sex was not always a part of their many meetings; it was not uncommon for them to share an evening together watching a video film, enjoying a quiet undemanding companionship.

'Sir, what do you want me to do?'

'You may have guessed that I am in one of the less well known branches of what used to be called "Intelligence" but is now known as Security. We have a problem and we think you could help us. Let me explain.'

The story that Sir Jacob told, when reduced to its essentials was this. Somehow drugs, hard drugs from the East or through the East, were being smuggled successfully into Britain and the money from the sales was being used to finance terrorists, particularly the IRA. A lead had indicated that the drugs might be coming ashore somewhere along the West Coast of Scotland. Before the lead could be exploited the agent who had discovered it had been killed. It had seemed at first an ordinary car accident but it was an accident too convenient to be unplanned.

'We want you,' said Sir Jacob, 'to take over and to trace the source of the lead, and if possible to discover where the drugs are being landed. All we have to go on is a recorded telephone message from Morgan before the accident, it said "I'm on my way to Oban – I'm in a café, this telephone's a bit public, then I'll catch the *Claymore* and . . . oh my God he's coming. Goodbye, darling. Give my love to the children and to dear old Eileen, Eileen More, she has the answer to your question." He then rang off. The accident took place half an hour later, he was run off the road, his car ended upside down in a loch, he was drowned. That's our problem: we have to find and talk to this woman Eileen More. But where do we look?' Sir Jacob stood up, and looked out of the window. 'Can you help, or rather will you help? I rather fear that there may be that rather fashionable animal in our organisation – a mole, so I feel that a fresh eye will help. That is why I am seeing you here.'

'Well.' Michael walked over to the window. Outside it seemed a pretty ordinary day – far out at sea some steamer was passing from right to left rather like Coifi's sparrow, and below men and women busy with living passed and interrupted one another, dogs paused at lamp posts and pillar boxes. One dog that should have been on a lead barked at a cyclist who wobbled dangerously for a moment then righted himself and turned to curse the animal's owner. A matter-of-fact kind of a day. He turned and faced the man behind the desk.

'May I ask you a question?'

'Certainly, what is it?'

'Sir, why and how me?'

Sir Jacob laughed. 'That is two questions, not one: but I'll answer them.' For perhaps half a minute, he said nothing. Only the ticking of the grandfather clock broke the silence.

'It's the old boy net: not the usual one. Your chief and I were boys together in the Portsmouth slums, we grew up together, stole together, won scholarships together, suffered the fools above us together. He went into business, I into the Civil Service, but . . .' here he paused, then went on, 'but we never lost touch, I use him as a priest, a confessor. I told of my dilemma, the presence and effect of a mole, my need for a new man, one without many ties, one who could dive, one of Morgan's note refers to diving off the Mull coast.'

Ah, Michael thought, that's why George asked me if I could scuba dive; but he knew already. Sir Jacob went on, 'George told me that he believed he had someone who might help. He'd been impressed with your work and the reports from your superiors. He told me your name and I had you carefully checked: pretended it was to do with the oil fields, checked out half a dozen of your colleagues to give the investigation verisimilitude. Does that satisfy you?'

'Yes, sir, thank you.' Michael felt easier now. He thought for a few moments and then spoke.

'What exactly do you want me to do?'

'Good, now here is a breakdown of Morgan's last week. We've built up a picture, pretty complete, of where he went and what he did. I now want you to retrace the steps and follow the same pattern. See if anything happens. This,' he held up a sheet of paper, 'contains the names of people he might have met and talked to. I want you to check them out'.

'All right, I'll do it – how do I keep in touch?'

'I'll give you a number: you'll have to memorize it, you can use it in an emergency.'

Michael was silent for a moment or two, then he looked directly at Sir Jacob.

'Sir.'

'Yes?'

'I think that I may know Eileen More.'

'What!'

'I think I may know who or rather what Eileen More is.'

'Good God.'

'You see, sir, I am a Scot. I know the West Coast pretty well, I have some Gaelic too. Eileen is the Gaelic for Island, Eileen Mohr means *big island*.'

'Go there then.'

'There is a difficulty, sir, I am afraid.'

'What is it?'

'Have you a map of the West Coast of the Islands, a large-scale map?'

'Yes, of course, but not here.'

'Well, sir, when you get back to your office, look at it and you'll see that there are a number of islands all called Eileen Mohr: can you tell which one your agent meant or shall I have to check them all until I find the right one?'

'That's a good lead, McNab, a bit of luck, good luck.'

'What shall I do now, sir?'

'Nothing: wait and we'll get in touch with you.'

'What about my return to work?'

'We'll deal with that, nothing for you to worry about: just go back to where you're staying and wait for instructions.'

'That's all, sir?'

'Yes, that's all, thank you. Good afternoon.' He stood up and pressed the intercom switch. 'Mr McNab is going now, please come and see him out.' He held out his hand. 'Glad to have met you, McNab, and thank you.'

He was halfway out of the room when Sir Jacob called him back: 'Hey, McNab, come back, here, you have to sign this.'

'What is it, sir?'

'Secrets Act, we all have to sign.'

'Very good, sir.' Michael scrawled his name across the page. Caught, he thought, snared, now no more than a spider's dinner. He shuddered slightly, he felt sick, his inside was churning.

That was that, McNab, Michael McNab had become, albeit temporarily and somewhat reluctantly, a British agent. He went back to London and waited.

Four days later he received his orders and left the South for the West Highlands, tracing a tributary back from the main river to its source. He caught the Highland express at Euston, Platform 14, pushing the trolley bearing his luggage down the sloping gangway to the platform. He found the First Class sleeper booked for him by the Department under the name of John McDonald. The attendant, a coloured man with a strong Glaswegian accent, came to collect his ticket and find out when he wanted to be called.

'You're getting out at Crianlarich, sir?'

'Yes.'

'When would you like to be called, sir, and would you prefer tea or coffee?'

'Six o'clock, please, even if the train is late, and tea please.'
'Very good, sir.'

Michael had a considerable amount of luggage for he had brought a wet suit, and for camouflage a fishing rod (not brand new), waders, a creel and a hat stuck with flies. Again not a new hat but one which even to the casual observer had obviously seen some service. The equipment had been bought at a small place in the backwoods of Kensington, recommended by Sir Jacob and paid for by the Department. He had always enjoyed fishing, at least in theory, but a certain squeamishness and an innate laziness prevented him from taking up the sport really seriously. It was taking the hook out of the fish's mouth that he really hated doing; he could not believe that the fish felt no pain.

He stowed his luggage, then descended to the platform; watching the passengers go by, hurrying to find their seats, worried looks, relaxed couples, a wonderful sample of ordinary people. The list of his sleeper companions was posted on the carriage door. Not all were taken. There was a Lt Col. W. Smith, a Mr and Mrs Gordon, Lady Dalmally, Allan Forrester MP. He looked at his watch, only three minutes to go. He climbed back on the train and went to his sleeper. A whistle blew: the train began to move. The journey, the assignment had started. He rubbed his hands together. Breakfast in Crianlarich.

CHAPTER FOUR

Interlude at Lord's

'In spite of all their kind, some elements of evil
Persist with difficulty here and there on earth'

SUMMER was eliding into autumn, shadows came sooner and were longer. There was a dustiness in the air; trees had lost their gleam, pitches were browner, tired, less springy: good cricketing weather. A taxi deposited an elderly gentleman at the Grace Gates. He wore a slightly crumpled linen suit, a London MCC tie, a panama and he carried an ancient air-bag and a copy of *The Times*. Other men also clutching bags and wearing binoculars as necklaces were entering the ground, flashing as they did so the small red card that proclaimed their membership of the MCC, the second best club in London.

When presented with a seemingly intractable problem, Sir Jacob would take himself to Lord's (that is if there was a match to watch) and, depending on the weather, position himself either in front of the Pavilion or on the upper level of one of the public stands at the Nursery end of the ground. Here, with a packet of sandwiches, a large Thermos of strong black coffee, real not instant, and a flask of malt whisky, he would allow the gentle rhythm of the match to provide the background against which the problems then troubling him would more often than not slip into solution. Usually during the break for luncheon he would make his way to the Bowlers' Bar to see whether any old friends were there. On this particular day, the morning session, Middlesex were batting, had been slow, undistinguished and uninspired, solid but utterly without grace or excitement, brawn plenty of it certainly but little sign of brain or style. What, he mused, had happened to style, has it really disappeared or is it simply that I am old? Do all old men dream dreams and shun reality? He spotted an elderly man (during the week all members tend to deserve this description) on his way out of the bar down the wooden stairs to the seats below, a tankard of beer in one hand, a copy of *The Times* folded to show the half-completed crossword in the other. Sir Jacob called out:

'Will, hold on, may I join you?'

'Morning, Jacob, boring isn't it?'

'Yes, tedious, but none the less I do find it relaxing.'

The two men settled themselves on the benches outside the Pavilion and took out their sandwiches, a couple of hopeful sparrows joined them, scavenging at their feet. The sun had disappeared behind the Pavilion, a gentle but not unwelcome breeze stirred the county flags over the dressing rooms. Seagulls circled the clock tower, screaming abuse at each other. The electronic scoreboard was flashing encouraging messages and county information. It was warm and pleasant, inducive of sleep.

'I have a problem.' A blunt unvarnished statement.

'Yes.'

'It is like this.' Sir Jacob then explained his dilemma. Although the mole in his Department had eventually been uncovered and, as far as was possible, the damage caused had been repaired, there was no, nor indeed could there be any, reliable or completely trustworthy guide to assess the extent of the harm that had been inflicted. The worst scenario would be that the names and positions of all members of his Department (it was a pretty small department) were now known to the other side; but who were the 'other side'? The days of post-war certainty were past, the Cold War was coming to an end, indeed was being replaced by the interlocking of terrorism with drug-dealing, drug dealers with the Mafia, the Mafia with certain national and international intelligence services, a complicated ever-changing dance, an international excuse-me in which partners would change with bewildering rapidity.

'Whom can I trust?' A rhetorical question.

'It's not only trust, is it?'

'No, I know, Will, what I really mean, or at least what I think I do, by trust is not personal individual loyalty, but how do I know that

INTERLUDE AT LORD'S

all my fellows are not being followed, their homes bugged – I know that I am followed. Probably.' Here he pointed at a stout, lame member in a slightly soiled blazer drinking double Bells's and addressing loudly all unfortunate enough to be within earshot.

'Could be, but I doubt it. I know him. I take your point, though.'

'I can't change all my chaps, can't afford to. Actually, lately I have taken on a new man only for this one case, not as a permanent member of the Department. He's not at all bad but, and here's the question, he came to see me in the office of a friend of mine in Brighton. I was there, had I been followed, and it is quite likely that I was, then he would probably have been marked as someone worth watching, do you see?'

'Yes, it is difficult. You can't, I suppose, disband the Department then re-form it. We did that to H-group in '64, if you remember.' Sir Jacob shook his head. 'Well, then, it looks as though you'll have to look elsewhere, find someone new – can you?'

'We could, possibly, but it would take time. I've no one in mind, nothing at the moment – do you know of anyone?'

'No, but I'll keep my eyes and ears open.'

The bell behind them on the balcony was struck by a steward, the luncheon interval was over. The umpires appeared and walked together to the wicket, short white coats, cloth hats, former county players equitable of temper and miracles of concentration. They fixed the bails on the stumps.

Sir Jacob got to his feet. 'Will you be here on the nineteenth?'

'Yes, I'll see you then – good luck!'

'Thank you, Will; ah, here come the players.'

The fielders clattered down the pavilion steps and through the gate.

Sir Jacob walked through the Long Room. The two batsmen passed him, helmeted and padded, looking and walking more like trainee astronauts about to test the moon's surface than eager young cricketers preparing to confront the imaginary danger of a medium fast seam bowler in his last season. Quite unnecessary, he thought. When I was a boy the bowlers were much faster, no one wore helmets or thigh pads then. What's wrong with them – no balls that's their problem, a poor pun. Everyone is getting soft. We're all soft now. He laughed as he walked back to his seat, remembering how when he was a boy his grandfather had made much the same complaint. What did he need? It looked, or so the information coming on to his desk seemed to show, as if before long he would have to send someone to Kenya –

Mombasa was well situated to be a drug centre, directly on the route from Asia to Europe and the dhows from Iran were impossible to control. He could, he supposed, borrow from one of the other departments or from the police, but this would lead to divided loyalties and divided command. He would need seriously to start searching. He sighed, for it was a tiresome exercise. I wonder, he thought, how that young man is getting on in Scotland.

He woke with a start. He had dozed off, made drowsy by two pints of beer and the warmth of the sun. He felt slightly sick. Damn, it's always a mistake to fall asleep in the afternoon. He pulled himself together and took out his Thermos. There was still enough coffee left for one cup, tepid but strong. It served to awaken him. He looked at the scoreboard. Good Lord, he had slept through four wickets and 68 runs. The talk with Will had helped, his mind was clearer. He knew what he would have to do. He would find someone outside, someone unconnected with his or any office of the security departments, not now but later and it would be someone he could send to Kenya if it were necessary to do so. Poor chap, he thought. Out there was some poor unsuspecting fellow enjoying his life, perhaps a little bored with the pacifity of the daily routine, but safe, unthreatened, a beautiful ripening peach waiting for him to pluck it. He grinned with pleasurable anticipation. He felt much better.

'Good shot.' Almost involuntarily the comment slipped out as the ball was beautifully middled. It streaked to the boundary. 'Well played. Well played.' Sir Jacob settled back to enjoy the game.

CHAPTER FIVE

Out Of The Deep

'Too many there be to whom a dead enemy smells well, and
who find musk and amber in revenge'

HAD it not been for Rory I would probably have been in Greece or even Palestine. The Frankfurt Book Fair was over; after it I usually went on to somewhere in the South, to recover from the noise and general turmoil, the frenetic activity of thousands of publishers in search of gold chattering like London starlings settling for the night. This year, however, I had promised Rory – it was his half-term – that I would take him to Tiree.

We drove to Glasgow airport, I parked the car and we checked in for the Logan Air flight to Tiree. Some people call the strange cigar-shaped plane that the airline uses a flying coffin, a name at odds with its impressive safety record. Rory was enchanted, he was excited as only a small boy can be. I could sense the energy building up. For him this was real flying, the airplane small enough to be understood, quite different from the huge Jumbo villages in which he had flown before.

Towards the end of October the hotel at Scarinish is pleasantly empty. It stands on one side of the little harbour, it was and indeed still is an old inn but it has been modernised and extended, and for me at any rate it has the great asset of a marvellously successful hot water system that provides at any time of day or night a seemingly inexhaustible supply of boiling water.

THE SCENT OF POPPIES

In late October the geese are beginning to fly in from the North, as well as flocks of redwing, fieldfare, and golden plover. I saw my first golden plover on Tiree. There are on the island few hills of any consequence, but there are plenty of bogs and if, which is not uncommon, it is wet, water lies in the ditches and fields. Snipe are common and a little later in the year sportsmen arrive ritually to massacre them – the hotel kept a record of the 'kill'. I had on several occasions before Rory's coming spent a few days on the island, either at the end of October or the beginning of November. I found the emptiness attractive and the feeling that one was on the edge of the world. Nothing as one looked westwards at the setting sun, nothing for thousands of miles until North America.

The beaches on the west are sandy and clean, the sea, depending on the sky, wine dark which I take to be purple (though I have never yet had a purple wine to drink, even in Greece), green, turquoise, emerald – translucent loveliness, impenetrable, clear. One looks for mermaids and mermen, for sunken cities, lost continents, for Atlantis, for Lyonesse, less romantically but more practically, for Spanish galleons, their holds full of gold coins and treasure waiting to be found and plundered. But none of these is to be seen. No mermen, but a seal would often come inshore to watch and listen, no Atlantis, no golden guineas but golden shells, cowries and scallop shells.

It is possible to hire bicycles and this I used to do, for one could then ride to the ends of the island and safely leave the bike against a fence or a wall and explore the beaches and dunes.

When I had booked I had checked that there would be a bike the size that Rory could ride. The distances were too great for him to walk with any pleasure, and I had no intention of hiring a car.

The sky was clear, only a few wisps of cloud floated beneath the plane as it made its way to Tiree. Below us were a sprinkling of islands: Mull, then Iona, Staffa to the right, and in the distance Lunga and the Dutchman's Cap.

'Look Rory, there is the Abbey; that hill is Dun I, at the top of it is the Well of Youth.'

'What's that, Uncle?'

'The Well of Youth? Under one of those large rocks there is a small pool, water collects in it; it is said that if you bathe your face in its water you'll keep your youth and come back again to Iona.'

'Have you?'

'Yes, I have – Do you know, one year it dried up, and another year

I found a skylark's nest at its edge; the eggs hatched before I left. One day, Rory, we'll go there, you'd love it.'

The airplane began to lose height, the descent had begun. The airfield — an old military one I think — lies in the flat centre of the island. Round its edge a number of buildings gently fall apart, and the concrete paths are veined with cracks in which wild flowers and grasses grow. A sleeve billows in the wind. A quiet peaceful place; a few vehicles, cars and small vans, waiting for the plane. We landed and disembarked. We had a short wait for the baggage to be unloaded. A car from the hotel was there to pick us up.

The hotel stands, as I have said, at the head of the harbour, which although it is not large provides a safe anchorage for small ships, for it is almost completely enclosed. The big steamers from Oban and Glasgow go to a jetty a mile or so to the north. An old wreck lies below the inn, at low tide its skeleton is exposed, a shattered ribcage of some vanquished giant. Our rooms were opposite each other in the original part of the inn; Rory's looked out over the sea, mine was at the back. He was delighted. I helped him unpack, then as soon as he had changed into old clothes he rushed down and out to look at the wreck at first hand. When I joined him some minutes later he had already picked up bits of broken shells and a piece of twisted, bleached driftwood.

'Oh, Uncle,' he said, 'this is jolly: I do like it here. What shall we do?'

I looked at my watch: it was not long to lunchtime.

'Well, I think that we might walk to the big jetty before lunch and see if the steamer is in. We can go along the coast and come back by the road. All right?'

'Smashing.'

We set off along the coast towards the monument that stands on the headland.

'Look, Uncle, look, mushrooms.'

True enough there were, the tailenders of the season. I always carry at least one plastic bag in my pocket and a Swiss Army knife, surely one of the most glorious gifts that that nation has donated to the male chauvinist world.

'Pick them, Rory, we'll take them back with us: I'm sure that they'll cook them for our breakfast tomorrow.'

The jetty was empty, the steamer, so we were told, had been delayed and was not expected for a couple of hours. A few parcels and crates were stacked waiting for loading. We walked back to the hotel by the road, stopped at the paper shop on the corner – we had to go in and buy chocolate and Rory wanted a postcard to send to Nanny and one for Sandy the doctor's son; then past the Police Station: one year I remember a friendly but ill-disciplined golden labrador from it joined me on an afternoon walk during which he indulged his addiction to sheep chasing! We reached the hotel.

'Ah, good, I need a pint, what'll you have – coke, ginger beer, lemonade?'

'Ginger beer, please,' then a pause. 'Uncle.'

'Yes, Rory.'

'Uncle, I'm quite hungry.'

'OK, we'll eat, what would you like?'

'Fish'n chips, please.'

I knew the man behind the bar, and after greeting him said, 'Could we have two fish and chips, please.'

'Certainly,' he answered, 'I'll just go and order it for you.'

'What shall we do after lunch, Uncle? Can we go for a ride?'

The trouble with small boys is that they are powered by engines that never seem to be switched off – the idea of silence and inactivity is utterly alien to them. Contemplation is another word if not for laziness then for old age: if you wanted to sit still then you were old. In a way this is true, but no one, certainly not someone like myself who pretends to a form of perpetual youth, likes to be reminded that one's hair is less thick than it was once, and one's waist measurements have ceased to be smaller than those of one's chest, the inverted isosceles triangle has become a pear.

'Rory.'

'Yes, Uncle.'

'Please, go up to my room and fetch the map of the island. I think it is on the top of the chest of drawers, if not it will be in one of the pockets of the haversack.'

'Aye, aye, Cap'n.' He had been reading, or rather I had been reading to him, *Treasure Island* and he lapsed sometimes into a version of nautical language, casting himself either as Jim Hawkins or as Silver – it depended on whether or not he felt in need of rebellion.

I spread the map out when Rory brought it down. 'Look,' I said, 'we are here and this is the north of the island. That's where we walked this morning. There's the airfield where we landed.'

'What's that? What's a vit, vitri-something fort?'

'Vitrified. It means that sometime in the past fire has caused the silicon in the stone or mortar to liquify and then run together, that's a bit complicated but when you heat sand it can become glass if you use really great heat.'

'Oh, Uncle, can we go there, please? I've never seen a glass fort.'

'I don't see why not if the bikes are ready.' The fish and chips arrived and were soon despatched.

The bicycles were ready, and after a little adjustment to the seat the smaller proved suitable for Rory. I warned him:

'Rory, please remember that there are a good number of cars on the island and that the drivers often think that there is no other traffic, sometimes too they are drunk, the worse for wear, and then they drive on the wrong side of the road or straight down the middle. So please ride properly, no show offs, OK?'

'Aye, aye, Cap'n!'

I was not wholly convinced by the seraphic smile. I had witnessed it and accepted it before, with disastrous results. I had found that the more seraphic the smile the more demonic the subsequent actions.

'Are you warm enough? Nanny said that you must wear that new thick sweater. Go and put it on.'

'It is "on", Uncle, look.' So it was. I carried a small rucksack in which were my binoculars, a tin of Elastoplast, a large bar of plain chocolate (Rory did not know this), and our anoraks.

'Good, let's go.'

We rode against a slight breeze, but the sun was shining and the air was clear and tasted clean. The great bay, Traigh Mohr stretched on one side of the road, the sea running over the sand leaving behind as it ebbed away a brown froth rather like the head of a glass of Guinness.

'Can we stop, Uncle, and go on the beach?'

'No, I don't think so, if we do this afternoon then we can't go to the fort.'

He thought for a moment.

'The fort.'

'Right, we turn left after the Old Free Church and cross the island, it'll be up hill a bit but not too steep.'

We turned up the road. Soon the land fell away on the right and below us was the sea.

'Hey, Rory, stop. I think we'll leave the bikes here and walk down to the shore and then along the coast until we reach the fort.'

'That's fine, Uncle.'

We left the bicycles propped against a rocky outcrop, and turned off the road and climbed down to the shore. It was a beautiful afternoon, the sun was shining and the bay was partly protected against the wind. I sat with my back against a rock enjoying the warmth. Rory scampered about, fascinated by the shells, stones and driftwood, searching for new treasures, seemingly completely happy.

'What's that, Uncle?'

'What's what?'

'Look, those grey things over there, are they seals like the ones at home?'

He pointed out to sea, to some rocks.

'Ah,' I said. 'Yes, they are seals, seals basking. Let's sit and watch them for a bit. I fished the binoculars out of the haversack and focused them on the seals. There were seven lying on the rocks and the heads of others bobbing in the water. We sat there, very still, sheltered and partly hidden by the rocks. I grew drowsy.

'Uncle.' Little more than a whisper. 'Uncle, look, what's that moving near the seals?'

I shook myself out of the half sleep and took the glasses and looked at the spot at which Rory was pointing. Something large, different in shape, blackish, was moving towards the beach. It was a frogman, someone in a wet suit.

'Sh, Rory,' I said. 'Keep quite still, don't say a word and don't move, just watch.'

The black shape took on a more recognizable form as it drew nearer to the shore. The figure stood up, shook itself and waded ashore, pushing back its goggles as it did so. He or she, more likely a he from the shape, took off his flippers. When he reached the shelter of the cliff he took a sack from behind a rock and then stripped off the suit. It was a young man wearing vest and scarlet briefs. He opened the black sack and took from it first a shirt, then trousers, a sweater, socks, shoes and an anorak, and lastly a small orange haversack rather like ours. Having dressed, he bundled up the suit and flippers and put them in the sack, which he then put in the hollow behind the rocks and covered with boulders. He stood up, straightened himself, lit a pipe, then putting on the haversack he strode away along the coast towards the path that led up to the road; we were hidden from his view by rocks.

'Rum. That, Rory, was very rum.'

Poor Rory was so excited that he had to rush behind a rock to spend a penny. 'Uncle, Uncle, isn't this exciting, it's a n'adventure.' Questions cascaded out, few of which I could answer either to his or to my satisfaction. He ran over to where the sack had been hidden.

'Shall we dig the suit up?'

'No.' About that I was firm. 'Let it be, at least for the moment. Have you a clear picture of the man, can you describe him? Could you recognize him if you saw him again?'

'Yes, of course I could.' Rory was indignant.

'Good, for I think that we'll meet him again soon, but for the moment let's go and explore this fort.'

The fort was a success, and Rory roamed round it and over it with evident pleasure: but I could see that most of the time the mystery of the frogman occupied his mind and to tell the truth mine also. What on earth could the young man be doing? There was probably a simple, innocent explanation but somehow I doubted it. He had not looked like a criminal, indeed he looked excessively healthy, clean and presentable. I looked at my watch.

'Soon'll be teatime, we'd better get back to our bikes.'

'This is a super place, Uncle, I do like it.' His pockets filled with shells and pebbles, his hair, as indeed mine was, blown and tangled, his face glowing with pleasure, he looked and indeed was a happy, carefree small boy. He took my hand and we climbed up the path to where our bicycles were parked. I paused for a moment:

'Look, Rory, I don't think we'll talk about that man coming out of the sea, we'll keep it secret.'

'Aye, aye, Cap'n.' He squeezed my hand in agreement. The ride back was mostly downhill and it was not too long before we were back at Scarinish. The sun was disappearing, there was a chill in the air, a sharpness: at this time of year, night fell quickly. When we reached the hotel we put the bicycles away in the shed and I went into the kitchen to see if I could rustle up some tea. In the hall stood two bulky brown-suited men in hats and coats. The landlord was speaking to them.

'You can have 14 and 15,' he said. 'How long will you want to stay?'

'Two days, perhaps, three, not more,' one of the men answered. He had a flat voice, metropolitan with a touch of the North in it.

'If you follow me, I'll show you your rooms.'

We settled in the warm sitting room by the open fire, tea came, hot and strong with a plate of fresh buttered drop scones which soon disappeared. There was a television set but the pictures were very poor, a lot of interference so we turned it off. A bookcase held books, games and some old magazines, the leftovers of the visitors. Rory had brought some paperbacks with him, also a large scribbling pad and some coloured pencils.

'I'm going to draw an island,' he said, 'with treasure and birds.'

'Any pirates?'

'Yes, pirates. I'll prob'ly put in a cave for Ben Gunn.'

He lay on the rug before the fire, tongue sticking out in concentration. I had bought a new Gollancz crime, an Emma Lathen. I find the character of John Thatcher, the Wall Street banker, immensely attractive. It was a peaceful time, I drank my tea.

'Uncle?'

'Yes, Rory.'

'Uncle, look, I've put in the seals and the man.'

He showed me his map and there on the sea stood the figure of the man we had seen. He had flippers on and goggles.

'Ah, that's good,' I said, 'but I think that perhaps we should burn it, we don't want anybody here to know about the man. It's secret, we shouldn't talk about it. Not until we get home – the map is so good that it would give the game away.'

Regret at the destruction of a masterpiece gave way to the excitement of being part of a real secret.

'Aye, aye, Cap'n. Please, let me do it.' He took the map from me and held it to the flames, watching them curl up at the edges, burning the paper to black and brittle ash.

'Burning a map of the Island, young man?'

The speaker was one of the brown-suited chunky men we had seen in the hall. He had come silently into the room. I wondered whether he had heard our conversation.

'No, sir, it is only a 'maginary island, not this one. My uncle has been making up a story for me about pirates and treasure.' The big man stood in front of the fire, and thrust his hands deep into his pockets.

'Capital place this,' he said. 'Capital, fine birds, eh? Good to get away from the City for a few days of rest and fresh air.' An unconvincing rather laboured attempt at conversation, or at least so I thought, but good manners demanded that I should answer.

'Are you interested in birds, is that why you and your friend are here?'

'Indeed, indeed, yes. Good time for geese, eh?'

Rory sat back on his heels and looked up. I felt something frightening would come out, so I hurriedly went on.

'We saw quite a number of interesting birds this afternoon. Rory is going to make a list of all we see, aren't you, Rory?'

'Yes, Uncle.' He turned to the brown suit. 'I haven't made a list yet for today, I've got to look in the book and identify some of them.'

'Capital,' he rubbed his hands together, 'capital.'

Rory returned to his drawing and I to my crime story. Brown suit sat down and took a newspaper, one of the tabloids, from his pocket and began reading; an uncomfortable silence descended. It was probably imagination but there seemed an intimation of disaster, impossible to distinguish, to isolate. Into this silence, breaking it and dispersing the sense of unease erupted Bonzo. Bonzo, the offspring of many illicit unplanned pairings, the image of one of those fabulous medieval beasts, head of a lion, body of an eagle, came into my mind – Bonzo was part labrador, part spaniel, part retriever, part sheepdog, the product of a mingling of countless different genes. He sat on Rory who squealed with delight, and Bonzo thumped his tail, knocking over crayons, books and the half-empty tea cup, part of whose contents went over the shoes of brown suit.

'Here, I'd better rescue that.' I picked up the cup and saucer and put them on the tray. 'I hope your shoes are all right.'

'No problem, I assure you.'

Bonzo licked Rory's face.

'Look, Rory, I think you'd better take that monster downstairs before he does any more damage. Why not put on your coat and take him round the harbour – don't forget your gumboots.'

'Yes, please.' As Rory led Bonzo away, he could be heard scolding him as they went downstairs.

'Nice little chap, your nephew.'

'Yes, Rory's fine, he likes dogs, we left our own at home, he misses him, I think.'

We talked for a little time. He seemed determined to discover who we were and what we were doing. I was equally determined to give nothing away. After a decent interval, long enough I hoped to remove any thought from his mind that I was consciously, deliberately, trying to avoid speaking to him, I got up and moved towards the door. 'I think I'll just go down and see what Rory's up to; with that monster to look after anything could have happened.'

The sun had set and the darkness had thickened as it had been swallowed by the sea – I walked round the edge of the harbour.

'Rory,' I called, 'Rory, it's time you came in.'

At my side, rubbing himself against my legs, the undisciplined body of Bonzo appeared. Hanging on to his collar was a panting boy.

'Uncle Adam, we saw a n'otter, at least I think it was, it was on the shore, but Bonzo frightened it, do you think it was?'

'I see no reason why it shouldn't have been, there are still quite a number of sea otters around these islands – I've seen them on Iona. But you are very lucky, it's another first, you can note it on your list, they're rare creatures now.'

'It was beautiful, Uncle.'

'Nearly supper time, we'd better go in and get ready – mind you wash your hands.'

'Aye, aye, Cap'n.'

Domesticity was not really my line, I had always been determined not to be tied down by possessions or over-burdened with responsibilities, but here I was clucking like an old hen, worrying whether my chick was clean! What is more, what is really so extraordinary was that I would not have had it otherwise.

Dinner. Dinner in the hotel. I was in the bar with Rory, he had a coke, of the taste for which I was in vain trying to cure him, I had a malt whisky. The door opened and the young man from the sea came in. He looked round and came to the bar.

'Good evening, sir, what'll you have?'

'Oh, let me think, a beer I think, a pint of bitter. You do have draught, don't you?'

'Yes, sir.'

The young man came and stood in front of us.

'May I join you?' he asked.

'Of course, do sit down – make room, Rory. This is Rory.'

'Hullo, I'm Michael.'

'Are you here for long?'

'A few days only, I'm on an island tour – like Dr Johnson – I work in the Middle East and am on leave, escaping from the heat and the lack of alcohol.'

'Oh, what do you do?'

'I'm a geologist, mostly oil prospecting now but when I was a student I spent a long vacation on Mull – the geology there is fascinating, it is so diverse.'

He fidgeted with the ashtray and beer mats – could not keep still.

'Good evening.' The other brown suit came in, Rory moved closer to me and felt for my hand.

'Two large whiskies and soda please.' The other man came in and joined his friend at the bar. He turned to the young man:

'Did I hear you say that you were a geologist?'

'Yes, I am.'

'Ah, that's interesting, why are you here?' A frontal attack.

'I am on holiday, I was just telling this gentleman that I am touring the islands, relaxing after a long stint in the Middle East.' Then turning the question round, 'And why are you and your friend here?'

'The birds, my friend and I are studying migration routes.'

The gong sounded.

'Good, time for dinner: come on, Rory.'

It is strange how, when recorded, the conversation of strangers meeting, the small talk, sounds so stilted, unreal, while in fiction beautifully rounded sentences conceal the truth that in real life people speak in half sentences and hide their feelings behind shrugs and silences. Literature is written, seldom spoken. *Hansard* now seldom records anything other than banalities and jargon. Days, weeks will slide by without a quotation sullying the uninterrupted flow of turgid verbiage. The literary allusion and erudition have been banished along with Fullers cake and trams.

CHAPTER SIX

I Meet Sir Jacob

'From ghoulies and ghosties and long-leggety beasties
And things that go bump in the night,
Good Lord, deliver us!'

IT was not until after nine, much later than his usual bedtime, that I had Rory bathed, in bed and read to. I was reading the *Jungle Book*s to him. When I had been a small boy, at home every evening my mother had read to me or told me a story; and in the early days of Rory's coming to me I had found it a successful way of establishing and maintaining a good relationship. He would lie curled up in bed and I would read to him a chapter or two of a book chosen by me. Tonight when I had finished and shut the book, Rory put out his hand and touched mine.

'Uncle?' he said.

'Yes, old chap.'

'I don't like that big man – do you?'

'No I don't, he's too nosey.'

'What does he want, Uncle?'

'I'm not sure but I think it's probably something to do with the seal man, wet-suit Michael. Now, he's an enigma.'

'What's a nigma?'

'An enigma not a nigma – it means mystery, a riddle, something hidden which we do not wholly understand, a mixture perhaps of all these – is that clear?'

'Yes, thank you. I think he's scary, like Kaa.'

'Yes, old man, rather like Kaa, but Kaa was on Mowgli's side. Anyhow, remember it's not our problem.'

I bent over and kissed his forehead.

'Good night, scamp, sleep well.'

He held me tight for a moment, for some reason reluctant to let me go.

'Good night, Uncle.'

'Remember, Rory, if you want anything my room is opposite. Now I'm going down to have a nightcap.'

'What, one with a bobble?' He giggled and relaxed, delighted with his joke.

I switched off the bedside light.

'Uncle, please don't shut the door.' This surprised me for Rory had never before shown signs of fear of the dark.

'All right, I'll leave it ajar, OK, is that enough?'

'Thank you, 'night.'

''Night.' I went downstairs to the bar for my nightcap and bobble.

A pleasant rumble of conversation greeted me when I entered the bar – it was quite full, some residents, others islanders. Michael was at the bar drinking whisky, it already seemed that he had had enough to turn taciturnity to garrulity. I ordered a malt whisky, Laphraoge. I was choosing a different malt each time, and there was a notable row behind the bar, several of which I had not heard of before. A peat fire smoked in the grate, a couple of islanders were playing darts. The two heavies were drinking Guinness, murmuring to each other. I sat down. Michael came and sat by me.

'I've just been putting Rory to bed: reading to him.'

'I loved being read to,' he said, 'it made one feel so safe.'

I noticed that the big man had edged a little closer, perhaps in order to hear what we were talking about, so I spoke rather more loudly than the occasion demanded so that he would not be disappointed.

'Is this your first visit to Tiree?'

'No, I was here several times as a child – three years running, my family used to take a house for a month in the summer, in those three years we got to know the island pretty well.'

'Care for a game of darts?'

'No thank you, not tonight if you don't mind, I feel pretty tired.

I'm just going up and then after a bath I'm to bed with a new thriller. It's been a long day,' he laughed, 'and so much fresh air.' He got up.

'Good night.'

'Good night.'

He left the room rather unsteadily. Very shortly afterwards one of the two heavies left too.

I had another drink and then after a short, desultory conversation with the man behind the bar I, too, went up to bed. Before going to my room I pushed open Rory's door. He was fast asleep. I shut the door gently and went to my own room.

I had a bath; one characteristic of the hotel, as I have previously observed, was that the water was always hot. I read in bed for an hour or two before turning out the light. The curtains I had drawn back earlier and the light of the moon shone into the room, a pale silvery light that was soft and gentle, touching the curtains and carpet with colour. The sky was splattered with stars glittering like diamonds on a velvet cloth. The sound of the waves beating on the shore was wonderfully relaxing. I must have been asleep for an hour or so when something woke me – I am a wretchedly light sleeper – and I shook myself into consciousness. The door handle was slowly turning. The moonlight was falling on the door and in it I could see the movement. The door opened very slowly and Michael stepped into the room bare-footed and wearing only scarlet briefs and a shirt and sweater. I sat up, he held a finger to his lips, carefully shut the door, painfully slowly so that there would be no click. He came and sat on the edge of the bed. He shivered.

'I must talk to you,' he said. 'I need your help.'

He began the story. It had not been hard, he told me, to find the various islands called Eileen Mohr but although he had searched he had found nothing, most were barren rocks rising sheer from the sea. He had found nothing until he had come a few days ago to Tiree and then he had been lucky. By this time in his telling he was shaking like an aspen leaf.

'Look,' I whispered, 'you had better get into bed with me or you'll freeze to death.'

He slid in and I felt his body against mine, his feet were cold.

'Your feet are blocks of ice.'

'Sorry.'

'Don't worry, go on.'

He had, he went on, found that on the island one of the deserted

I MEET SIR JACOB

abandoned cottages was called Eileen Mohr – apparently some Englishman had bought it in the late thirties and had so named it in an exercise of ignorance. His name incidentally was not Waggett.

'But why the wet suit?' I asked.

'Oh that,' he said. 'I was not exploring the islands, I was visiting lobster pots.'

'Why?'

'I'll come back to them – I have discovered that this cottage may be used as a staging post for the drugs, but I'm not sure, absolutely sure, whether it is for drugs coming in or for drugs going out. What I think may happen is that the drugs come in by sea from trawlers or tankers and are then sent south in the lobster boxes.' He went on: 'You see, they collect the live lobsters from the pots all along the coast and keep them alive at Eileen Mohr and then they are sent to Glasgow and from there flown south to London and France. No one would think of opening boxes of live lobsters to look for drugs, would they?'

It seemed feasible enough.

'But why tell me all this?' I asked. 'Why don't you ring Sir Jacob up and tell him.'

'I can't,' he answered, 'the lines to the mainland are out of order – I've tried this afternoon, the post office are "looking into it".'

'But why don't you fly out tomorrow, or catch the steamer?'

'I was going to try, but, you see, these two men who arrived today will kill me or try to kill me if they see me either at the airstrip or the jetty.'

'Look,' he said, taking a piece of paper from the top of his underpants, 'I have made a list of all the addresses to which the lobsters go. I want you to take this and hand it personally to Sir Jacob. I am sure these are the distribution centres for the drugs.' He took the crumpled letter and handed it to me. 'Please take this message to Sir Jacob, and tell him what I've told you, tell him that I think that the most important link is M'Fish of Green Street.'

'The fishmonger?'

'Yes, that shop.'

'Very well, you convince me. I'll do what I can, but what are you going to do?'

'I thought that I would try to escape from the island. There are fishermen and crofters with boats, I'll try to get a lift to Coll, I'll leave here in the early hours before dawn.'

'Don't you think, though, that you may be over-reacting, over-dramatising what is happening?'

'No, I'm not. Remember, they have already killed a man, my predecessor, there is an enormous amount of cash involved and it's not only money, terrorists are involved and they're ruthless, death means little to them.'

'Right,' I said, 'I'll help you. You stay here and I'll lend you a spare pair of trousers and another sweater and . . . what size shoes do you take?'

'Tens.'

'Mine are ten and a half but two pairs of socks will fix that – now try to get some sleep.'

He was asleep in a few moments: I woke him some hours later – asleep he reminded me much of Paul when we first met.

'Wake up, Michael, time to go.'

Michael dressed quickly in my clothes, I gave him the bars of plain chocolate I had.

'Now, out of the window, quickly.'

My window was about twelve feet from the ground, but the roof of an outbuilding was below the window.

'Goodbye and good luck.'

He put his arms round me and gave me a great hug.

'Thanks,' he said, 'we'll meet again.'

'That's a promise.'

He was gone. I went to make a diversion. I switched on the light and stumbled about the room, then opened the door and went down the landing to the lavatory. The door of one room was ajar, I thought that I saw someone or something move but could not be sure. Another door opened down the passage, only briefly – good, I thought, both were looking inwards. This would give Michael a better chance to get away. I stayed a few minutes, pee'd, then pulled the chain and padded back to my room. After a minute or two I put out the light. I fell asleep and dreamed not of robbers, or killers or spies but of digging potatoes in my grandfather's garden. The old gardener came to see what I was doing, I was only eleven. He put his hand on my shoulder. 'Now, now,' he said, 'you've done enough.'

'Wake up, Uncle, wake up. It'll soon be breakfast time.'

Rory was shaking me by my shoulders.

I struggled to awareness, my watch showed it was nearly eight.

I MEET SIR JACOB

Rory was fully dressed, even his hair seemed to have been brushed, he seemed consumed with excitement.

'What is it old chap?'

'The police are downstairs, two of them, something's happened, everyone's rushing about. Do get up, Uncle, please.'

I was fully awake. Rory was sitting on my legs.

'Be a good chap, Rory, and let me get up.'

'Aye, aye, Cap'n. I'll check on the Fuzz.' He threw a punch at me and fell off the bed. He was gone.

It did not take me long to wash, shave and dress.

Downstairs the sergeant and a constable were talking with the proprietor.

'What's happened, what's the matter?'

The sergeant turned and looked at me.

'Good morning, sir,' he said. 'I trust you slept well.'

'Yes, thank you.'

'Did you hear anything in the night, sir, anything outwith the usual, any noise?'

I pondered this question and paused before answering.

'Er, er, no, I don't think so, why?'

'Well, sir,' the constable broke in, 'the gentleman in number 8 seems to have disappeared.'

'Disappeared, no, how do you know? Perhaps he's just gone out for a walk. He said he was interested in birds, and was here to look at the geese and duck.'

'No, sir, no. When Mr Swerling took his tea up this morning he found two rather strange things. One, the bed had not been slept in and, two, the room had been ransacked.'

'But how could he tell about the bed?'

'Although the room was upside down the bed was still tucked in, even though it had been turned over.'

The story when pieced together was that someone, some person or people had ransacked, 'done over', Michael's room and that Michael himself had disappeared – the island is not small and it would not prove too difficult for someone to find a safe hiding place. What I did not tell the sergeant was that I had a good idea where Michael had gone and how he had gone probably by wet suit, although in this I was wrong. Rory was almost unable to contain himself, he found it difficult to finish his breakfast.

'No,' I said. 'No.' I was determined that I would not, at least for the time being, tell Rory what had happened in the night.

I was perturbed by what Michael had told me and I also was convinced that it would not be long before the two tough men turned their attention to Rory and me. We would have to get off the island, but how? It would have to be today. I began to devise a plan: we would go to the west bay and take a sandwich lunch. I ordered the lunch and I packed a haversack, a bit fuller than normal. I also scribbled a letter to Swerling which I put in my pocket. We set off watched by the larger of the toughies.

'Off for the day?'

'Yes we're exploring the west – taking our lunch with us.'

'Have a good day.'

'Thanks.'

I knew that the 'plane left at 11.30; and Rory and I did not stop at the west bay but rode on to the airport. I stowed our bikes and gave the letter to the officer on duty. I said in it that we had been called away unexpectedly and would be grateful if his wife could pack our cases and put them on the next available boat to Oban. I enclosed a signed blank cheque.

I was on tenterhooks until the plane took off – there were only two other passengers. We strapped ourselves in. From the window the airport seemed calm and undisturbed. The plane circled the airport then set course for the mainland. The sky was clear of clouds and the islands below were green jewels ringed by deep dark seas. One of them was Iona, that most magical of places where the boundaries between the present, past and future are so thin that it seems sometimes that a mere puff of breath would scatter them. Mull. The mainland. Hell, Rory. What should I do?

'Thank God, Rory: we're away – I'll tell you about it now.' When I had finished Rory said:

'Gosh, Uncle, it is an adventure. What do we do now?'

He had listened quietly while I told him about Michael's escape in the night; and a partly edited account of the drugs and the murdered agent.

'We, Rory? No, not we, you're going back home, I'm going to London.'

The problem was that once it was discovered that we had left the island, the two men would get in touch with their mainland HQ and almost certainly a connection would be made and someone or indeed several people sent to look for us. Probably someone would even now be on their way to Glasgow — but how could they send a message when the telephone lines were down? A lucky break for us. But they might have a short-wave transmitter. What should I do with Rory, how could I get him to the village while I went to London to see the man Michael had told me about?

Rory voiced his objection.

'Uncle, why can't I come with you to London? I could stay in the flat, couldn't I, please?'

I had been thinking that this was a possibility but I was not sure what I would do with him when I had to be away from the flat. In any case, I wondered whether it would be safe to stay there, my address was no secret. 'Well,' well always presages a weakening, a sign that one is about to change one's mind. Rory sensed this and he smiled, that joyful smile that lit his face when he was especially happy. I still found it strangely moving that he should be capable of so much happiness — that the wounds of the loss should have healed apparently so completely and that he should have found in me an acceptable surrogate father, mother, family. And me, what of me? This man who had thought himself to be reasonably self-sufficient was happily encumbered with a child not his own, to educate, to comfort, and perhaps above all condemned to share everything with. Sharing makes so many demands. It is easy enough to pay school fees, the butcher's bill, and for riding lessons, but to share time, to have to be in most evenings if not every one, not to be able to indulge in pleasures that one had thought essential for one's well-being — these I had happily jettisoned; at least for the moment. He was so vulnerable.

'All right, Rory, all right, I give in, you can come to London with me.'

I began to tell Rory about Iona. 'You know, Rory,' I said, 'in early June Iona is one of the most beautiful places I know. There are hidden inlets not often seen by the ordinary visitors, they can only be reached when the tide is out or by clambering down almost sheer cliffs, following sheep paths among tufts of thrift and bloody cranesbill. Oh, Rory, you would love it, we'll go next year.'

'Go on, Uncle, please tell me more.'

'In one of those bays there grows a wild white rose, it's called a Burnet rose and it has a scent so gentle, so sweet, it is so fragrant, so delicate that one feels that it must be one of the sweetest on Earth. When one lies basking in the sun, often a buzzard passes overhead quartering the territory looking for carrion or rabbits.' For some moments, it seemed only for a few but in fact it was for over five minutes, I was silent. Land passed underneath.

The flight by now was nearly over, Glasgow was below us.

'Now, listen, we must move quickly, we have only a few minutes to get to the London Shuttle: luckily we've no baggage.'

We landed and hurried to the gate for the London plane; we made it just in time. What were 'they' doing? Did 'they' see us board the aircraft? There was sure to be someone at Heathrow to meet the flight and to follow us. How could we recognize them? I settled back in my seat to think about ways and means.

I discovered later that our departure had not been noticed until lunchtime, and that even then no message could be sent because the telephone connection was not restored until the next morning. We rose above the clouds, Glasgow was blotted out.

'When we get off, Rory, I want you to pretend that you are with someone else, not with me. I think that then we'll take the Underground. I'll get the tickets, you follow me and meet me at the barrier.'

The shuttle soon reached Heathrow, it circled and then landed and we made our way to the centre part of Terminal I pretending to be strangers. Rory came down the gangway first, chattering to a motherly-looking woman. I followed some twenty passengers behind. We were not, I believe recognized; indeed, there was no one there watching, the elaborate subterfuge had been unnecessary. Having no luggage to wait for we were able to go straight to the Underground station. I bought tickets and was joined by Rory at the barrier. We went through together and boarded the train.

'They' would, if by now our absence had been observed, have alerted their London representatives and my flat would certainly now be watched. I had decided that I would ring my doctor, an elderly man of infinite wisdom with a large house in Hampstead, and a garden. He was a widower and was looked after by a married couple. She, the cook-housekeeper; he, the chauffeur-valet. We got out at Gloucester Road and changed trains, taking one to Baker Street. From here I telephoned the surgery.

'Could we stay?' I asked.

'Of course,' came the answer. He would telephone Rosa and warn her of our imminent arrival.

I MEET SIR JACOB

'Thank God, Rory, you'll be able to stay with Theodore and I'll be able to get in touch with Sir Jacob.'

'Uncle?'

'Yes.'

'I'm jolly hungry.'

'All right, we'll eat.'

We crossed over from the station and found a fast-food café. I hated them, cardboard food and tasteless tea-bag tea. Rory loved instant junk food and chips, always chips.

'What are we going to do now, Uncle?'

'Well,' I looked round the café, the only other people besides us were two young men in paint-stained overalls and a sad-looking middle-aged woman with a full shopping basket sipping a cup of tea and gazing into space, her lips moving silently in some secret conversation. It all seemed peaceful enough.

'Rory, I must find a telephone now and ring Michael's Sir Jacob.'

We went back to the station and I found an unvandalized telephone and dialled the number that Michael had given me. I heard the bell ringing at the other end; it was answered almost immediately. The voice at the other end repeated the number.

'Good afternoon,' I said, 'I should like to speak to Sir Jacob.'

'Hold on for a moment, sir.' Then. 'Who is it speaking, please?'

'My name is Adam Masson, I've a message from Michael McNab for Sir Jacob.'

After a moment or two a voice came on the line.

'This is Jacob Menzies – you say you have a message from McNab?'

'Yes, it concerns Eileen Mohr, it is necessary that I see you.'

'Very well, where are you.'

'At Baker Street station, in a call box.'

By this time darkness was falling and the street lamps were lit. The station clock showed it was 4.35.

'You know the Church, St Marylebone's Parish Church, it's opposite Madame Tussaud's?'

'Yes.'

'Well, meet me there, in ten minutes.'

'How shall I know you?'

'Don't bother, I shall know you: goodbye.'

The receiver was replaced, the line was dead.

Rory and I left the station and crossed over the Euston Road by Madame Tussaud's. When we reached the top of the church steps we found that the door was shut, so we had to stay outside. It was a little while before a small, nondescript car drew up and an elderly man got out. He came up the steps two at a time.

'Masson.'

'Sir, good afternoon, this is Rory.'

'How do you do, sir,' Rory held out his hand.

Sir Jacob laughed, and shook it.

'How d'y'do, young man. I think we'd better go to my office; come on.'

The car had those black windows through which the occupants can observe what goes on outside but which renders them invisible.

I am not sure even now exactly where Sir Jacob's office was, I rather think it was in one of those new buildings in the hinterland behind the British Museum. It was fully dark when we arrived and we were whisked up to his office on the top floor.

'Sit down, sit down.' He turned and pressed a bell at the side of his desk. A young personal aide appeared.

'David, would you please take this young man to the canteen and feed him, then show him round, he might like to see the rifle range.'

'Very good, sir.'

Rory stood up, gave Sir Jacob a formal bow and put out his hand and lightly touched my arm. He followed the aide out of the room.

'A credit to you.'

'Thank you, sir.'

'Now, what do you know?'

'Michael asked me to give this to you.' I handed him the letter. 'It contains a list of the possible distribution centres.'

'Thank you.' Sir Jacob read the list and put the papers in a folder on his desk.

'Go on, tell me what happened.'

I told him what had happened on Tiree. Sir Jacob listened, made notes and occasionally asked me to repeat or expand something that I said. When I had finished he nodded, 'Very good, very good.' There was a silence, it seemed endless. I ventured a question.

'Sir Jacob, what news of Michael, has he escaped?'

Another silence, then:

'Yes, actually he did escape and he has telephoned; his story coincides with yours. Now he's in hiding. I've sent people to Tiree.' He walked over to the window, turned round. 'Yes, we sent them by Naval helicopter to see what had happened. The two brown-suited

I MEET SIR JACOB

gentlemen left by steamer earlier this afternoon. The address in the register turned out to be an Edinburgh hotel. My men are still there.' Sir Jacob paused in his pacing.

'Come back tomorrow, will you? I'm not quite ready, have you somewhere to stay?'

'Yes, we have.'

'Give me your address and I'll send a car to pick you up at 9.30 tomorrow – now you'd better go there.' He rang the bell and a secretary appeared.

'Find David will you and ask him to come back here.'

A black, rather sinister car took Rory and me to Theodore's home. His housekeeper had been appraised of our visit and all was ready. Rory by this time was looking distinctly weary. We waited in the study, a smokeless fuel fire burned in the grate. Rosa had poured a large Scotch for me and a glass of milk for Rory.

He came and climbed on to my lap.

'Uncle,' he said, 'this adventure, what's going to happen?'

'I don't know, old chap, I really don't, but we'll find out tomorrow, I expect.'

I told him that Sir Jacob had heard from Michael, and that Michael had escaped and was now in hiding.

'Where?'

'He did not say, I suppose it is a secret.'

'Can I tell Sandy?' Sandy was his friend, the doctor's son.

'No, not Sandy and not Nanny either, at least not yet.'

I murmured on and then became aware that Rory was fast asleep. He looked angelic. I must have dozed, for suddenly Theodore was standing before me.

'Well, what's all this about?'

'Hullo.' Rory stirred and snuggled closer to me.

'I think,' I said, 'I had better get Rory to bed, then I'll tell you.'

I undressed Rory and got him safely to bed, supperless. If he woke, which I doubted, he would be able to get something to eat if he wanted it. Then I went downstairs and joined Theodore. He had refilled my glass.

'It's a queer story, Theo, listen.'

I outlined the story. Theo listened.

'You know,' he said, 'the growth in the number of drug addicts is quite frightening, and it really does seem as though in many instances there is a link with one or other of the terrorist organizations. One of my patients is a Home Office Under-Secretary and he tells me that the drugs are sold to raise the money with which to buy arms and explosives. They don't care, but I see some of the addicts and it is heartbreaking. I get very angry.'

Next morning the car arrived on time to pick me up and take me to Sir Jacob's office. Sir Jacob seemed in good spirits.

'Good morning, Sir Jacob.'

'Sit down, we have a great deal to discuss.'

'Is there any more news of Michael?'

'Yes, we've been in touch again. I've ordered him to lie low for the moment: too many people will be looking for him.'

'And the two men?'

'Ah, they seem to have vanished. We lost touch soon after they left the steamer. I've no doubt my men will soon pick them up. But there has been an interesting development. Just listen to this. When my men were searching the hotel rooms of those men they made an interesting and very lucky discovery. They noticed that in one of the rooms a window had been wedged with a folded piece of paper, obviously to stop it rattling. Well, they looked at that paper wedge. It was a folded envelope, on it was a name and address, quite legible. The address was Mrs E. Moore, Pendragon House, Dalmally, Argyllshire. We made inquiries and found that Mrs Moore is a widow, with two grown-up children. No one was in the house, a neighbour told our people that she had gone to stay with a sister in Kenya.'

I was impressed. 'You must have moved very quickly, sir.'

'Not bad, we can move pretty fast when pushed, and I've got men up there.'

'But,' I said, 'what about the cottage, it had the same name – is that a coincidence?'

'It might be, but I rather think that they chose that cottage because of its name. There were others empty and just as suitable; it doesn't really signify, one of those strange quirks when fact takes it stance from fiction.'

Sir Jacob, who never seemed to sit down, paced up and down the room while he was talking.

'What else, sir?'

'We discovered that her husband had been a specialist language officer attached to the British Council, he was based just before his death at one of the Middle East offices.'

'How did he die?'

'Officially an accident, he was a keep-fit fanatic and while on a secondment in Cairo he used to take a skiff out on the Nile before breakfast. One morning when he was passing Gezira his craft apparently hit something and overturned. Although he was a competent, indeed some would say an expert swimmer, he drowned. We don't know whether or not he was trapped under the skiff or whether he developed cramp, but he was dead by the time he was rescued by a passing fisherman, and at the autopsy our doctor found nothing – but we are pretty sure that he was killed.'

'But do you know why?'

'I'm sorry but that's something I can't tell you, the information is classified.'

I said nothing, indeed I did not know what to say: silence provokes confidences. Sir Jacob stopped pacing, he looked down at his desk, and picked up a sheet of typescript.

'Your father still lives in Kenya,' more a statement than a question.

'Yes.'

'Would you,' he paused, 'would you be prepared to go out there and visit him, for a couple of weeks or so?'

'Well, I usually go out to Kenya on business at least once a year, as I'm sure your people have discovered, and I haven't been this year yet, Rory's presence has prevented it.'

'Yes, well, we would like you to go to Kenya, on the pretext of visiting your father, and then find Mrs Moore, watch her, observe her friends and talk to her.'

'Why me? Haven't you your own men you could send, departmental staff who are trained for this kind of thing?'

'Yes, but then again, no – we can't do this at the moment, will you go? We shall of course pay.'

What should I do, what decision should I take? I should like to go, especially at someone else's expense, but then what about Rory, what would happen to him? I couldn't take him to Kenya with me, nor would I want to. I could always leave him with Nanny, she wouldn't mind moving in for a fortnight or so, and Rory was happy with her, or I could always arrange for him to stay with friends of mine. But he would not like me going away for so long.

'What about Rory?' I asked.

'Rory, ah yes, we have considered that problem, what we would be prepared to do is to send one of our junior staff to stay in your house.'

'Rory's not a problem.'

My protest was brushed aside as of little or no importance: on reflection that is perhaps an unfair comment. Rather it was that to Sir Jacob Rory's situation was an impersonal matter that could be dealt with by administrative action, no mental exertion was needed. Sir Jacob made a great effort and wrenched his mind from speculation.

'Masson, now look here, don't think we don't care we do, perhaps sometimes too much.' He pressed a bell and the young man who had taken Rory under his care yesterday came into the room.

'David, you met Mr Masson yesterday.'

'How do you do, sir.' He held out his hand, I took it, it was a strong confident grip.

'Thank you.'

'David is the man I am thinking of allocating to the job of being Rory's minder whilst you are away.'

'All right,' I said, 'I'll go, but I really am determined that Rory should be consulted first. If he is too upset by the idea then I won't go.'

'Good, well now you must tell him, but before you do so let us make some decisions about your story, it must sound true and credible.'

'Very well.'

'Firstly, David. I think that we should pretend that he is some sort of distant cousin who has been rather ill and is in need of a longish period of recuperation and relaxation in the Highlands – some sort of breakdown perhaps after an unsatisfactory love affair.'

'Look,' I said, 'before going on I really do want to speak to Rory, could David go and fetch him – I'll telephone and tell them that a car is coming for him.'

'Excellent idea.'

I telephoned Theodore's house and it was not many minutes before Rory arrived. He seemed already to be on excellent terms with David. Sir Jacob left us alone and I explained to Rory that I had been asked to go on a special visit to Kenya, that my excuse was that I had to see my father, that unfortunately I could not take him with me, and that David would, while I was away, be staying with him and Nanny at the cottage. But I also told him that if he really would rather I did not go I wouldn't. Rory looked very solemn. He was unconvinced.

'Uncle?' he said.

'Yes.'

'Is it dangerous?'

'I don't think so, but it may be, I think it is just a fact-finding mission, not an active one – not cops and robbers.'

'I like David.'

'Yes, he seems a nice chap.'

'I suppose you'd better go,' he looked very woebegone, very fragile but perfectly determined.

'Thank you, Rory, I'm grateful.'

Sir Jacob was delighted when I told him and he thanked Rory.

But I was still unhappy, a little doubtful. I had responsibilities: what would happen to Rory if I were killed. I had made a will leaving the guardianship to an old friend who had three children, all round about Rory's age. But this was not an answer only a solution. Would he see through the 'David ploy' and, this was perhaps the most important consideration, would he be in any danger, any physical danger, caused by my decision? I havered but in the end I convinced myself. One thing that I would have to do would be to speak to Nanny, and explain to her that I had been called unexpectedly to see my father, and that Cousin David would be coming to stay for some weeks. How would Nanny take this? – she knew my cousinage better than I did. To tell the truth I was a little jealous, jealous that this fit and attractive young man, David, much nearer to Rory in age than I am, would by his athletic prowess, by his very youth, displace me in the boy's affections. Not that I was physically unfit, I could and did play 'hard' and Rory would often throw himself at me, like a cheetah kitten with its parents, and I could and did bowl interminably at him – but I was middle aged and youth has an inbuilt attraction, a strong magic difficult to combat, almost impossible to rival. But the risk had been taken.

'Whose son?' Nanny had asked and I had invented an imaginary uncle and aunt, courtesy titles for old friends of my father's. Being a wise woman and having brought me up she sensed that there was behind the simple meaning of the words a hidden and far more important reason.

On the second day we went to Sir Jacob's office, collected again by the blackened car. This was to be the day of parting. A passport, a new one, was waiting for me, mine was locked up in my flat and we were pretty sure that 'they' were now watching the flat. I was to go the following evening on the BA flight. I had the day before telephoned my father and told him that I was coming, and I asked him to arrange for me to be collected at the airport.

Rory and I were in a small room next to Sir Jacob's office.

'Well, old chap,' I said, 'the time has come for you to go to Scotland and me to Kenya.' Rory did not say anything. 'David will take you back and will stay with you until I get back. Now, remember, not a word to anyone, not to Nanny not to Sandy, it's our secret.'

Rory looked up at me, a look of loneliness, almost of fear, on his face.

'Uncle, please don't stay long, I'll miss you.'

'No, old chap, I'll try not to.'

I lifted him up and hugged him.

'Don't cry, Rory, it's not for long, and I promise I'll telephone from Kenya.'

'Can't I come too, please?'

'No, I'm afraid not.'

Why couldn't I take him, he would get on well with my father, children did, and the farm would be a wonderful place for him but, no, it would be useless to try to persuade Sir Jacob to change his plans.

'No, Rory, it can't be done.' I put him down and taking out a less than pristine white handkerchief wiped his eyes. I knew that I was deserting him; whichever way one looked at it I was leaving him behind.

'Uncle, you will be all right won't you?'

'Of course, why ever not?' But he knew that the mission was connected with danger, with the man who had come from the sea, with the two men in the brown suits.

David came into the room. He looked at me, then at Rory.

'Sir, I think we ought to begin moving if you don't mind.'

'Right, now, Rory, please, go with David, give Nanny my love and Cracker too, and send me a postcard.' One more frantic hug.

'Aye, aye, Cap'n,' then turning to David, 'I'm ready.'

I was alone, the room was still and empty. No sound, the windows were double-glazed. I realized for the first time that in this room, this office, one could hear nothing of the outside world – no sound of traffic, of striking church clocks, of police sirens and car horns. Sir Jacob came back into the room, rubbing his hands, those prehensile hands with their matted covering.

'Your ticket, travellers' cheques, and other documents are ready. Miss Flower has them next door – goodbye and good luck, keep in touch, you've this number.'

I shook the proffered hand.

'Goodbye, sir,' I said, and then added, 'you will look after Rory?'

'Of course, of course we will, don't worry, David is with him.'

In the outer office I collected the papers and checked when I had to be at the airport the next day. Among the papers was a book, a present from Sir Jacob. He had written an inscription:

> Pray for a brave heart, which does not fear death, which places a long life last among the gifts of nature, which has the power to endure any trials, rejects, anger, discords, desire . . .

The book was a first edition of *The Shropshire Lad*. An enigmatic choice. The rest of this day I spent buying new clothes and avoiding old haunts where I might have met people I knew. I even went to an afternoon film show, the first I'd been to for three years. In the evening Theodore and I dined in and played chess. He beat me – twice. A becalmed moment before the wind came over the horizon.

CHAPTER SEVEN

A Labour of Moles

'The pickled salmon,' Mrs Prig replied, 'is quite delicious. I can partick'ler recommend it. Don't have nothink to say to the cold meat, for it tastes of the stable. The drinks is all good.'

'WHAT do you know?'
'Not very much, I'm afraid.'
'I thought so.'
The grey-haired elderly lady, neatly and well, but not too well, dressed (her shoes were excellent), who sat opposite me in the wine bar was Sir Jacob's messenger, although it would perhaps be more accurate to describe her as an envoy rather than an actual angel.

The wine bar, squeezed between a sex shop on the one side and a fast-food restaurant on the other, situated in the skirts of Soho where the Chinese area merges into the burger and cinema belt, was for the moment a favourite meeting place of the Department. There are a number of such safe restaurants which for a time are patronized. The other regulars become used to the man with the Magdalen college tie or the woman with the blue shopping bag and tinted glasses, until one day a regular would remark:

'I have not seen that chap lately, you know the one with the Magdalen tie.'

'No, must have changed jobs.'

The owner, a New Zealander, was usually frenetically present, and the food and wine were streets ahead of the normal wine-bar standards;

fresh and well cooked, well served in the first case and carefully and knowledgeably selected in the other.

At one end of the bar at lunchtime during the week there was usually gathered a group, predominantly male, of various occupations and ages, a strong contingent being of somewhat vociferous and opinionated members of the MCC, whose opposition to the cricket establishment had become a matter of principle.

'What do you know?'

Was that the right question, would not some other have been better. 'How much do you know?' or 'Do you know why you've been chosen?'

Miss Carpenter, for that was her name, had worked for the Department and its predecessor in one capacity or another since the latter days of the war. For many years before her retirement she had been attached to one of the small but exclusive Mayfair *couturiers*, one which the wives and hangers-on of many of the foreign representatives would often patronize, and whose visits might, often in fact did, necessitate a visit to the Embassy or flat for a fitting. Her cover since her official retirement was that of a part-time book-keeper to a small but well-endowed charity.

She contemplated the glass of Madeira before her, dark and slightly oily-looking, then took a sip and dabbed her lips with a white handkerchief.

'Mr Masson,' she said, 'the problem is that not only is the Department undermanned – it always has been – but the incidence of crime has increased and is increasing, especially of the crimes connected with hard drugs.'

I had a mouth full of prawns, and could not interrupt.

'Moreover,' she went on, 'we have had, as Sir Jacob I think told you, a laborious mole, and although she – yes, it was a woman – was eventually discovered, we do not know accurately, nor with any certainty, the extent of the information that has been passed on, what is available to our opponents; whether, for example, the names of all the operatives have been disclosed. Poor Charles was taken out at Loch Awe, a victim of the betrayal.'

'Who are they?'

'Yes, I suppose you should know that. The mole was non-political, neither Russian nor Chinese. The motivation was financial not ideological, suborned by representatives of the drug cartel, paid for and manipulated by the so-called barons of Colombia.'

'Um, what do those people want to know?'

'My dear, isn't it obvious – you see references in the press to the continued action and investigation against the drug dealers, combined action of the police, customs, the special branch, the international agencies; well it is information about the combined plans, about proposed actions, it is this information they need to know if they are not to lose millions.'

She filled my glass with Australian chardonnay, somewhat heavy but pleasant enough, with a high alcohol content.

'Thank you.'

'Yes, she was, for some time, able to keep the syndicate informed about both the short- and the long-term plans, exercises and operations of the different organizations; it takes, as I am sure you appreciate, a little time to set up and co-ordinate joint special operations.'

'Good morning, ma'am.' A tall, shambling, middle-aged man in a green, slightly worn barbour, a copy of the *Independent* under his arm, nodded to her as he passed the table on his way to the bar's end.

'Good morning . . . the size of the profit that the terrorists receive', she went on, 'is enormous, but it is not only this that motivates us, but also the knowledge of the damage that the drugs can do, the wrecked lives, the sordid deaths, the spread of Aids, and the corrosive corruption. Sometimes one feels like one of those seven maids.' She paused.

'Why?' I asked. 'Why is it really necessary for me to go to Kenya? What on earth can I do that one of your trained experts can't accomplish?'

'I don't know, but at least I can make an educated guess – you aren't known as a company man, you have a legitimate reason for visiting Kenya and for staying there for longer than a tourist's visit, your local connections are excellent, but the real reason perhaps is that we don't know either the strength of the organization in Kenya or the people involved. In time we could, of course, find out – and the local government organization is excellent, but limited by lack of money and trained manpower – but we haven't really enough time. Too much is being planned and our information is that not only is there a major delivery planned soon, but plans are already laid for the expansion and the establishment of a strong Kenya organization – and with the kind of money available, this will result in government corruption and instability.

'Yes, I understand, or at least I can appreciate that there is a case for sending someone – but why me, could not someone else have been recruited?'

Miss Carpenter smiled, she sat back. 'My dear, it is just bad luck for you. You turned up. You really chose yourself. Sir Jacob regards it as an excellent example of serendipity. Would you like coffee?'

The moving finger had written, there was no possibility of rewriting the stanza, the tributary had joined the main river.

CHAPTER EIGHT

The Kenya Connection

'What to do there? says everyone'

I WAS obliged to travel first class. Both the club and the economy classes were full. I checked in, passed through security, paid for and filled in an insurance form and posted it to myself in Scotland. I went to the duty-free shop and bought a bottle, a large bottle, of Glen Morangie, then made my way to the Monarch Lounge. The stewardess on duty noted my name and flight number. I hung up my coat, put my bag on a seat and then went and mixed myself a long and strong campari and soda; and sat down to read the evening paper. Out of the corner of my eye I saw the telephone. I could ring Rory.

'Hullo, 236.' It was Nanny's voice, calm and safe, a hundred years away, infinitely reassuring.

'Nanny, Nanny, hullo, it's me, is Rory there, is he all right?'

'Of course he's all right: your cousin is a very kind young man, today he took Rory fishing – Rory,' she called, 'Rory, come here, your uncle's on the phone.'

'Uncle, uncle, we've had a splendid day, I caught a huge trout – two pounds – Nanny's cooking it for all our suppers. David is nice, we're going on the hills tomorrow.'

'Rory, be careful please, nothing stupid.'

'Yes, Uncle. Uncle!'

'Yes?'

'I do miss you.' My heart stopped.

'Good night, old chap. I must go now – they're calling my flight. I miss you too: very much.'

'Good night, Cap'n, good night.'

I put down the receiver, I felt alone and abandoned, and collected my bag and coat.

'Goodbye, sir.'

'Goodbye,' I answered.

The long walk to the departure gate, the checking in, the waiting to board, by the time we boarded my thoughts and emotions were well under control.

'Good evening sir.'

'Good evening.'

'Let me take your coat.'

'Thank you.'

The great advantage of travelling first class is that for someone who is tall there is plenty of room to stretch one's legs. The stewards treat one as an individual not as just another seat-filler, they are also more polite, solicitous. The food is better, far less plastic, the drink flows freely and one is unlikely to be surrounded by over-parcelled garrulous females. Also one is able to remain oneself – not squeezed or bludgeoned into becoming part of a jolly mass of sweating humanity burdened with too many fractious children, too many clothes, and far too much luggage. I value this opportunity of being myself almost more than any of the other advantages. I seldom watch the film; if I wear the earphones it is to discourage conversation. It sounds curmudgeonly, and I suppose it is by the present-day fashion which seems to glorify community and group activities and denigrates individuality.

I woke early, before first light; the cabin was in darkness. I fumbled in the airbag and found my washing kit and a battery razor. By the time I had shaved and washed the cabin lights had come on and the crew were preparing breakfast – easily the best meal on a plane.

The first streaks of light had cracked the sky – morning had broken when we landed at Embakazi. The new airport building is far less friendly than the old one; there, all was in one place, one did not have miles to walk.

'*Hujambo,*' I said to the immigration officer as I gave him my passport, '*habari gani?*'

'Welcome, sir,' he answered, 'how long do you wish to stay?'

'Three weeks, please.'

He stamped my passport, handed it back. 'Have a pleasant stay, sir.'

'Thank you,' I answered and moved on to wait for the luggage to come through. This always seemed to take such a long time.

When I had spoken to my father I had told him that my story was that he had asked me to come out because he was feeling rather under the weather and had important business and family matters that he needed to discuss. He had grunted a little but had agreed that he would let it be known that I was coming at his request. I promised that I would explain the reasons for all this to him when I saw him. Nonetheless he was delighted that I was coming for he wanted to talk to me about my young half-brother Andrew. Andrew was waiting for me, twenty, fair hair bleached almost white by the sun – in the modern fashion we hugged one another.

'Hullo, Adam, good to see you.'

'How's Dad?'

'Dad, oh, he's fine, complained about being tired the last few days, nothing much though.'

He spoke with a slight nasal twang – not unattractive, certainly not as unmusical as the regular South African accent.

He led the way to the car, a Citroen, and we loaded my luggage.

'I thought we'd stop at the Norfolk for breakfast, better than Muthaiga.'

'Good, I'll enjoy that.'

We drove to the city, Andrew chattering happily away.

'Andrew, what are you going to do?'

'Me?'

'Yes, you.'

'I don't know, I enjoy working on the farm but as you know it's not what I'm really interested in.'

'What's that, painting?'

'Yes, painting – I want to paint – I'm coming to Europe soon, Dad's promised me that I can.'

The road from the airport is a good one. Where it passes the Game Park, at the entrance a few cars were already queuing to get in. On the telegraph poles hawks sat watching the verges or preening their feathers; a white thick mist hung above the open land; this would disperse once the sun rose higher in the skies. A few cars carrying early workers into Nairobi passed us and a bus rattled by on the other side – nothing seemed to have changed since my last visit more than a year ago.

It is very pleasant to be remembered; the staff at the Norfolk greeted me with wide grins, handshakes and a strong and friendly *'Jambo, Bwana'*.

'No,' I said, 'I'm not staying now, perhaps later, we are just here for breakfast.'

Sometimes at home on grey dismal winter mornings when I am feeling gloomy and out of sorts I think of Norfolk breakfasts, I conjure up memories of those splendid meals.

'I think I'll book in for a couple of nights next week, I have work to do in Nairobi.'

I felt much more at ease; how very pleasant it was to be back. Andrew went to telephone Dad and tell him that we would soon be setting out for Naivasha.

'We'll go by the new road, the escarpment road is bloody awful, the potholes are worse than usual, the last rains have washed a lot of dirt away.'

'Andrew – ' we were on our way out of Nairobi on the way to the farm, 'Andrew, have you come across a Mrs Moore, she's visiting her sister, the archaeologist Cordelia Coombes?'

'I know Cordelia Coombes, she's now a Lake Naivasha resident, she has a guest bungalow in the garden of the old Thompson estate, she's up at Lake Turkana at the moment – but Mrs Moore, I don't think so, Dad'll know I expect. Wait, though, there was a red-headed woman, very striking, at a party last week, that might have been her, she was very mature.'

The heavy mist that in the morning so often blankets the edge of the escarpment and obscures the view of the Rift and makes driving hazardous was dispersing as the sun rose and soon we were able to look across that magnificent and largely unspoiled stretch of country.

My father was waiting for us, standing on the verandah, his old chief steward Ali by his side.

'It's good to see you, Adam, you look well.'

'Hullo, Dad, how are you, are you better?'

He laughed, 'I'll tell you later.'

'Hullo, Ali.'

'Jambo, Bwana, welcome.' We shook hands.

Some years ago my father had sold the old farm at Molo to a Nairobi-based company and had bought a much smaller estate bordering Lake Naivasha. Naivasha had in fact become something of a 'Little

England'. Those old settlers who, like my father, had 'stayed on' but who had neither the stomach nor energy to run their former huge estates and ranches had sold up and had invested in smaller farms or houses round Lake Naivasha. The climate was good, they could still play at farming, mostly growing vegetables for the overseas market and producing milk and eggs for Nairobi. It was a good, uncomplicated life and gave the farmers an occupation. They usually kept horses, there was even a riding school, very popular with Nairobi weekend visitors. These settlers, or I suppose one should call them white residents, used the Lake hotel rather as a club, gathering there in the evening, and sitting chatting on the lawns and in the bar, exchanging news and gossip. There was also a good swimming pool at the hotel used by Andrew and his friends as well as by the hotel guests – it was on the tourist route, and mini-bus loads of camera-bedecked eager travellers would periodically be disgorged. They brought work to the area and a breath of the outside world.

The lake is a wonderful place for birds: fish eagles sit in the trees and kingfishers hover over the water. In it hippopotamus wallow and blow, making feeding forays to the shallows and weed beds. The lake is full of fish, rich with food. Round the edge of the hotel's jetty there were many little crayfish, the herons loved these and fished for them all round the lake, and of late years there had appeared a new visitor: the coypu. Some had escaped from a breeder a few years ago and had since then bred in profusion.

Two days after my arrival Andrew and I were lying on mattresses having tea by the pool. Dad had gone to Nakuru on some local business. I was half asleep, my book had fallen off the mattress, in the trees birds flitted backwards and forwards chasing insects. Andrew nudged me. 'Hey,' he said, 'she's coming over here.'

'Who?'

'The woman you were asking about, at least I think she is.'

I sat up and stretched, picked up my book, and turned as casually as I could towards the entrance, through which was coming a woman of noticeable beauty. She must have been at least forty, her hair was deep auburn, that colour that can never be caught from a bottle, I thought of Cleopatra's barge. I guessed that her eyes were green.

'Do you know her?'

'No, not really, I told you I met her at a party last week but then I did not know her name.'

Behind her, following her into the pool enclosure was a middle-aged man, moustached, his shorts identified him as a resident.

'Who's he?'

'Oh that's Dave Hall, Major Hall, he grows vegetables for the UK market – beans mostly but some courgettes and peppers as well.'

I sensed that Andrew did not really much care for Major Hall.

'What's his background, who is he?'

'I don't really know, someone said he came out here during the Mau Mau uprising, with the British Forces, he liked it here, married a local girl and came back when he left the Army – not awfully popular, knows too much and wants to know too much – his wife died a couple of years ago, there were no children. He only moved here to Naivasha a few months ago.'

'Come on,' I said, 'let's swim,' and dived into the water; Andrew followed me and we spent some minutes racing one another. Then we climbed out, near where Hall and Mrs Moore were sitting, one of Dad's old friends was talking to them.

'Adam,' he called, 'come here, I want you to meet someone.'

'Eileen,' he said, 'this is Jonathan Masson's son Adam, just out from England. Andrew I think you have met.'

'How do you do?' We exchanged pleasantries.

'Why are you here,' she asked, 'on holiday?'

'No, my father's been a bit under the weather lately and as I had a quiet patch at home I came out to see him. I think he's probably been doing too much.'

'Are you staying long?'

'No, not long, probably only a couple of weeks – and you, are you going to stay long?'

'I don't know, a month, two, even three, there's nothing at home to take me back,' she laughed, 'only the winter, so it depends on whether I grow bored or outstay my welcome.'

'Do you live near London?'

'No,' there was a slight hesitation. 'No, actually I have a small house in the Highlands, it was my husband's. It is very peaceful up there, I use it as a retreat – my children use it too, when they want a rest.'

'Are they here with you?'

'Good heavens no, Elspeth is at Bristol University, she's going to be a vet, and Ronald is a cadet in the Merchant Navy, he likes travelling.'

'Would you like a drink?'

'Yes, that would be nice, may I have a brandy and soda please.'

'I'll just put on my clothes I think.' I slipped into the changing room and put on my shorts, then went to the bar to order the drinks.

In countries like Kenya that bestride the equator day very quickly elides into night – often at this time, especially after the rains, insects come out and, attracted by the artificial lights, descend in their thousands on house or hotel, making life impossible. A beer in which several *dudus* – such is their Swahili name – have drowned themselves or a whisky into which a moth has nose-dived are neither universally enjoyed nor relished.

This happened now, soon after the steward had brought our drinks.

'I think we had better go in, don't you?'

'Yes, certainly.'

We moved across the lawns to the hotel and took ourselves and our drinks safely behind the gauze. Eileen Moore on the surface appeared to be a charming and intelligent woman, well informed, well read, and with that ease of manner that is so often the hallmark of the wealthy. It seemed that in the absence of her sister, digging up our ancestors by Lake Turkana, she had attached herself to Major David Hall – was there, I wondered, any significance in that?

'Adam,' Andrew, who had been talking to some younger friends at the bar, came over to where we were sitting, 'Adam, I think that we'd better be making tracks, Dad will be expecting us and he's got the new DC coming to dinner, sorry to break up the party.'

'Right you are,' I turned to Eileen Moore. 'I'm sorry that we have to go, but I do so hope that we meet again.'

'Of course,' she said, 'do please keep in touch, you know where I'm staying; your father must bring you over to dine.'

We left the hotel. Andrew was uncharacteristically silent – when we got home he said, as he got out of the car – 'I don't like that woman – I don't trust her.'

CHAPTER NINE

The Mugging of Michael

'There is no substitute for wool'

W<small>HEN</small> Michael had climbed out of my bedroom window at Tiree he was undecided where to go or what to do. One thing that he had to do was to get in touch with Sir Jacob as soon as possible. He remembered where a call box stood in the village. It was no surprise for him to discover that even though the lines had been out of order some one was taking no chances for the wires had been cut. He made his way out of the village. By great good fortune outside one of the houses a bicycle leaned against a shed. He 'borrowed' it and cycled briskly off, not quite knowing what he was doing or where he was going. He stopped and relieved himself. The moon was waxing: there were few clouds so it was not too difficult for him to keep to the road, the country was open, trees were rarities, mostly nestling in sheltered hollows or in the lee of hills and buildings. The eyes of creatures unidentifiable in the pale light punctuated the verges of the fields and the sound of the waves pounding the sands of Traigh Mohr provided an acceptable soothing musak.

When he reached the cluster of houses at the north end he parked the bicycle against a wall and settled down in the shelter of an outbuilding; he ate some of the chocolate that I had given him. He shivered and fell asleep.

The first rays of the rising sun threw fingers of light across the sky, and Michael became aware that he was awake, cold and hungry. He needed to do something. Lights went on in a nearby cottage, first upstairs then down. He decided to take a gamble; he stood up and brushed himself down. He went to the cottage door and knocked. Inside a dog barked.

'Down, girl, down,' a male voice, not distinctly Scottish. He heard footsteps, then cautiously the door was opened.

'Yes?'

'Please, may I come in? I need help, your help.'

The door opened wider and Michael saw the man, well-built, in his later forties or early fifties, slippered, unshaven, tousled, a dog at his heels. The man looked at him for some time, then the dog, a sheep dog, moved her way round the man's legs and sniffed at him. He held out his hand and, her tail wagging, she rubbed herself against his legs.

'Meg seems to like you, come in.'

Michael entered the house and followed the man into the kitchen.

'I'm just making myself a cup of tea, will you take one?'

'Please.' Michael walked round the table and stood by the stove and warmed himself.

'Sugar?'

'Two, please.'

The tea was strong, thick and sweet; he swallowed a mouthful, he felt much better, life began to return to his numbed limbs.

'That's good: thank you.'

'Now,' said the man, 'what's this all about?'

How should he begin? The truth or fiction? He decided on balance for truth.

'I know that it is hard to believe, but I am on a special security mission, you could check but I think that all lines to the mainland are out of order.'

'Aye,' said the man, 'I tried last night, couldn't get through to my daughter in Norwich.'

Could he trust him? What other choice was there? There was none, so hesitantly Michael explained briefly what had happened.

'So you see,' he ended, 'I need to get off the island quickly and quietly. I can't use the wet suit because the oxygen cylinders need recharging, the sea's too rough for me to attempt to swim to the mainland or another island without oxygen. Can you, will you help?'

The man poured himself another cup of tea, it was even darker than before, stewed, he put three spoonfuls of sugar in it, stirred it and took a great gulp. He looked at Meg lying across Michael's legs, her tail blissfully beating the ground.

'Yes, I will.'

The man was not an Islander by birth but his wife was. He had been a craft teacher in an inner city comprehensive before his marriage, now he was an odd-job man, an electrician. He worked on his wife's croft. He grew vegetables and kept bees and fished and put out lobster pots. He had a boat. His wife was in Norwich with their daughter and the new grandson. 'Look,' he said, 'I can't take you to the mainland, it's too far for my boat,' he paused and drank some more tea, 'but I could take you to Coll, just over the water, how would that be?'

'That', said Michael, 'would be fine, I can then get to the mainland by steamer, and I am sure that I would be able to telephone from Coll.' The man offered him more tea, it flowed from the teapot like a Kenyan river after the long rains.

'You'd better have something to eat. I'll see what we have.'

What he had was rather stale sliced Glasgow bread, and slices of cold boiled bacon – he made Michael a couple of sandwiches.

'Take these with you, eat them on the boat.'

'Can I take the bike?'

A longish pause, then 'Yes, I don't see why not, look – I'll lend you another sweater and some mittens, you'll perish as you now are: and you'd better have this old rucksack of my son's. He took the rucksack from a cupboard, it smelt faintly of fish.

'Thank you.'

The sea was calm, there was little or no wind and it was dry. The crossing was uneventful. Michael ate his sandwiches crouched in the bow of the boat shivering despite his three sweaters. It was bitter cold despite the early sunshine.

The boat touched bottom and the fisherman waded ashore pulling the boat up the beach. Michael leapt ashore, dryshod. The fisherman went back for the bicycle.

'How can I thank you?'

'Don't, I believe your story – outrageous as it was, and Meg trusted you, she's an infallible judge – Goodbye.'

He held out his hand.

'Goodbye, thank you – you'll tell me your name, won't you.'

'Harold, Harold Norman, it doesn't signify.'

No one on Tiree could understand why months later in the Birthday Honours list the odd-job Englishman received an MBE for services to the State. He never enlightened them, refusing to answer all questions. He had eventually told his wife of the adventure, for she had been suspicious on account of the missing sweater which had been returned in a brown-paper parcel!

Michael waved goodbye to Harold Norman and watched for a time as the boat drew away, then he mounted the bicycle and rode away from the beach, past the castle towards the north end. No one was about, the stillness seemed to enclose him. After he had been riding for twenty minutes or so he reached a telephone box – at least, he thought, now I can get in touch with London. He dismounted and got through to the operator.

'Good morning,' he said, 'I want a reverse call to London.' The comfortable unhurried Scots voice took the number and within half a minute he was through to Sir Jacob's office, in another half minute he was talking to Sir Jacob himself. He made his report.

'So you're rumbled but you've disappeared?'

'Yes.'

'Right, go to the hotel, book in for a week, do nothing, ring me this evening.'

'Yes,' then, 'I've no clothes, no money.'

'We'll deal with that, we'll phone the local bank, is there one?'

'I've no idea.'

'We'll check, don't worry. Money will soon be on its way.'

It was not easy to follow this advice. How could he concoct a story that the hotel would believe? To appear at the only hotel on the Island on a bicycle with no luggage except an old rucksack would need some explanation. He remembered the old advice 'never apologize, never explain' and he remembered too the natural reticence and good manners of the Islanders.

The hotel stood on a little promontory. Michael propped his bicycle at the side of the porch and went in, no one was at the desk. He rang the bell. After some moments a pleasant-looking woman appeared. She looked surprised.

'Good morning,' she said.

'Good morning, could I please have breakfast and,' he paused, 'a room for a couple of days or so.'

'Yes, sir, that'll be all right, have you come far?'

'From the mainland – some time ago.'

'Will you sign here please, sir.'

She pushed the register at him, what name should he use? He decided on his own, less trouble in the long run.

After a good Scottish breakfast, Michael went out to look around. There was, as far as he could see, no store where he could equip himself, but there was a bank. When the bank had been open for a little time Michael presented himself and once he proved who he was he was able to draw as much cash as he wanted, this made him feel much more relaxed. Indeed, so exalted had been the man at the end of the telephone and so insistent that every assistance should be given to Mr McNab that nothing was too good for Michael.

There was little to do while waiting for instructions from London except to sit in the hotel; he could go neither for long walks nor rides, Sir Jacob was adamant that Michael should be on call. He spent considerable time in the bar, where he met a remarkable woman, the widow of a General. Her son had been killed on service in the Falklands, she was a nature artist of great skill and delicacy, and a pianist, locally much loved and, even more, respected. A woman he felt to be trusted and confided in; and she was delighted to have an audience to whom she could expatiate on the efficacy of honey.

'Is there', he asked her, 'any way of getting off the Island except by the steamer?'

'Why, are you in some trouble?'

It had taken her no time to understand that he wanted to avoid using the steamer where disembarking passengers at the other end could fairly easily be watched and identified.

'Angus could take you.'

'Angus?'

'Yes, he's a fisherman, usually pickled but the best I know, in a boat sober or drunk he's safe, I'll speak to him.'

'But where will he take me?'

'Across to Fionphort or Bunessan on Mull: you can land there and then go by bus or taxi across the Island to Craignure and from there take the ferry to Oban – from Oban onwards you should be all right.'

When she had gone, he rang London, and outlined the plan to Sir Jacob.

'Shall I try it?'

'Yes, not a bad idea of hers, thank her will you. I knew her husband, magnificent shot, bloody bad bridge player, trumped my ace.' The General's widow had been delighted.

'Now,' she said, 'you need kitting up. I've got some men's clothes in the house – my son's, don't you know – come over with me and I'll see what we have, you're near John's size I think.'

The clothes fitted well enough: he found an old tweed jacket, well cut with leather patches at the elbows, a superior sort of anorak, padded, a couple of shirts, a clean pair of grey flannels; his own jeans were by now stained and grimy.

'If you give me the jeans I'll get Morag to put them in the washing machine.'

'May I change now?'

'Of course.'

He changed his trousers and handed the jeans over.

Socks and pants he had been able to buy at the local shop.

That evening the General's widow appeared with the clean and pressed jeans.

'I've seen Angus,' she said, 'he'll take you for twenty pounds: tomorrow if this weather still holds, it should, the forecast is good.'

'I'll go, when?'

'Angus will be here in half an hour, you'll be able to discuss details then.'

'Thank you, I'm really most grateful.'

'Don't bother, but if you really want to thank me when all this is over, come back and tell me what really happened, will you?'

'Yes I will, I promise.'

'Michael, be careful.' In the brief time that had elapsed since she had met him, the numbness, hidden from the world by custom and the tradition of five generations of Service ancestors, that had deadened her affections had seemed to lessen. It was not that she no longer mourned the loss of Johnnie, a victim of Exocet; rather, as seasons gradually merge and winter's bareness as the days lengthen sends forth green shoots, so she felt under the warmth of a new friendship the stirrings of a seasonal change.

'Come back,' then she was gone.

Angus arrived, almost on time, a mere ten minutes late. Michael bought him a large whisky and then a pint of mild. He seemed ageless, his face dark as heather, veined a myriad times, rivers of purple blood criss-crossing it, a greasy woollen hat pulled low down over a few wisps of grey-red hair. Hair sprouted thick and abundant from ears and nostrils and on the back of his hands. He wore blue dungarees and a thick darned navy sweater and wellingtons. His blue eyes were watery – with alcohol. A few blackened teeth showed when he grinned, which was often.

Michael found it difficult to understand what he said, his accent was broad, his language flowery, full of strange metaphors and antique words. Somehow sense was made and it was decided that next morning, the tide being right and weather reasonable, they would set out for Mull.

'I'll be at the jetty at 8.30, Angus, see you then.'

Angus who was on the fourth whisky mumbled something that sounded favourable and then turned his attention to the barman.

The morning was fine and cold and it was growing light when Michael made his way down to the jetty. Angus, although he had been very drunk the previous evening, was already there waiting. As Michael descended to the boat he heard a voice calling him.

'Michael, wait, Michael.' It was the General's widow.

'Here,' she said, 'Morag has made you some sandwiches and here's a flask of coffee; you'll need it, Angus only has the hard stuff, don't you, Angus?'

Angus grunted and cast off.

'Goodbye, good luck.'

''Bye and thank you.'

'Come back, don't forget us, come back.'

Slowly the boat chuntered out to sea, the Island drifted away, he felt extremely unlike Bonnie Prince Charlie. Had the Prince, he wondered, been as cold and miserable as he now was when he had sped over the sea to Skye? He probably had been but then he probably was not fully sober, certainly he would have been thoroughly well wrapped and cosseted.

After half an hour he ate the sandwiches and drank a cup of the hot, sweet and strongly laced coffee, Angus had refused both – but he took, occasionally, a pull at a black unlabelled bottle. Michael smiled at the black bottle, it made him think of Cardigan and the Cherry Bums. That had been a splendid film.

Dutchman's Cap, Lunga, Staffa, Iona, then Mull – the boat slid into Fionphort, the village on the west coast of Mull which an American tourist not unoriginally but inaccurately once called the 'Gateway to Iona', it was the place from which the Ferry went to Iona. Had the tide been right they would probably have gone to Bunessan, as Angus was planning to go there and stay with a distant cousin, a spinster with a reputation as a cook.

THE SCENT OF POPPIES

'Thank you, Angus, I'm very grateful.'

Angus grinned, there was no need, he said, he had enjoyed the voyage. Now he would visit the old ferryman before going on later to Bunessan. He held out his hand, Michael took it.

'Go well,' said the old man. 'God be with you.'

'Thank you,' he answered. 'Thank you, Angus.'

Michael left Angus by the boat and walked from the landing place to the waiting room. Here there was a timetable: in one hour there would be a bus, the last that day. There was a tea room, it was warm and empty. He bought a couple of bars of plain chocolate and a cup of coffee. He chatted to the girl behind the counter; she came round and joined him.

'You know,' she said, 'although you'll get to Oban tonight, your train will have gone, you'll have to find somewhere to stay the night.'

Here was a dilemma, if he stayed in Oban there was always the possibility that by some unlucky chance he might be recognized by one of the watchers.

'You know,' the girl went on, 'you could always stay at Craignure and go to Oban on the first ferry.'

'That's not a bad idea, it is certainly worth considering, thank you.'

A number of other passengers arrived and the girl returned to her position behind the counter. The bus came, he boarded it, and settled back in his seat. By the time that they reached Pennyghael Post Office and The Clansman the light was failing and in the warmth of the bus he fell asleep, waking only just before Craignure was reached. Michael got up and paid for his ticket.

'Where's the hotel?' he asked the driver.

'Which one?'

'I didn't know there was more than one, what do you suggest?'

'Well there's the Craignure Arms or the new hotel just down the road; it might be easier getting in there, it stays open throughout the winter.' Michael decided to try the new hotel. The night was fine and the moon shed her pale light on the bare trees and calm waters of the bay. He walked to the hotel about a quarter of a mile down the road, the quietness and beauty wrapped itself round him.

He entered the hotel and booked a room; the room looked out over the bay.

'Have you a newspaper?' he asked the porter, and a day-old *Telegraph* had been produced. There was not much news; politics tended to bore him but there were some reports that held his interest, the sighting of a sea eagle in Dorset and a notice of a special exhibition at the Academy. He realized, suddenly, that he was exhausted, the events of the last few days were taking their toll. Dinner was some time off, he would take a bath. He began to undress, there was a knock at the door. 'Wait a moment,' he pulled his trousers back on.

A woman was outside the door.

'I've brought some tea, sir, Mr McNeil thought that you'd welcome it,' she entered the room and placed the tray, which held a pot of tea and a plate of buttered pancakes, on the table.

'Thank you, that's just what I wanted, please thank Mr McNeil will you.'

'Of course, sir, thank you.'

He lay in the steaming bath, the tea tray by his side, for well over half an hour, ate the pancakes, they were freshly made, and drank cups of sweet, strong tea (which normally he hated). Gradually he began to let go, properly to relax, warmth and well-being spread through his body. When he got out and wrapped himself in the large white towel he decided, somewhat reluctantly, that he ought to report to Sir Jacob. There was a phone in his room, but if he used it he would have to go through the receptionist, and even though he was convinced that he had thrown off his pursuers he wanted to take no unnecessary risks. What day was it? He had lost count of days, Wednesday was the day he had fled to Coll, today was Saturday, tomorrow was Sunday. No trains on Sunday from Oban, he might be able to stay another day here, that would be marvellous, he would suggest it to Sir Jacob. He dressed.

Downstairs, he went into the phone box and rang London, all he got was a duty officer, no Sir Jacob, he left his number and wandered, a little disconsolate, into the bar. Only one other person there besides the barman; an elderly man on the wrong end of middle age who was seated reading a book and drinking an outsize whisky and soda. Michael walked to the bar.

'What'll you have, sir?' asked the barman.

'Oh, – malt whisky please, which ones have you got?'

'GlenMorangie, Glenfiddich, Glen Grant, McCallan, Laphraoge.'

'That's the one, Laphraoge – a large one please.'

'You here for long, sir?'

'Probably a couple of days or so, not more I think.'

'What are you doing, sir, on holiday?'

'Er, yes, I'm researching a book, a thriller, and I need a certain amount of local colour. I know this area in spring and summer but not at this time.'

'It is different, sir, people who have disappeared during the season suddenly emerge – I'm not local, I'm from Buckinghamshire!'

'Really.'

'Yes, sir,' he was well away, the potentially dangerous discussion on what Michael was doing had been steered to safer un-mined waters. The flow of the barman's narrative was interrupted by a neat waitress who held two menus, one she gave to the seated man, the other to Michael.

'Would you like to order, sir?' she was away.

'Thank you,' Michael studied the menu, the waitress returned after a few minutes.

'I'll have the soup and the fish, can I order a bottle of wine?'

'Joseph has the list, sir.'

He chose a hock.

When he was half way through his meal, the receptionist came in, 'There's a call for you, sir.'

'Oh, thank you.' He rose and walked out to the 'phone booth. As he had guessed, it was Sir Jacob.'

'Well?'

Michael explained that he could not come south until Monday.

'I could, sir,' he said, 'either get the Monday sleeper from Crianlarich or go through to Glasgow earlier and fly to Heathrow. What would you like me to do?'

'Take the Crianlarich train; we'll book you a sleeper.'

There was a pause, then, 'Under the name of Saltburn, James Saltburn.'

'Why Saltburn, sir?'

'Eh? based there, briefly, in the war, bloody dull place – report on Tuesday, 'bye.'

'Good night, sir.'

The 'phone was put down firmly the other end.

He went back to finish his meal.

That night he slept deeply and peacefully, knowing that the next day there was nothing to do, no commitments – it was his, his only. Sunday was a glorious day, the sun shone, he got up leisurely, ate a huge and most satisfying Scottish breakfast and then went out for a four-hour walk. He got back tired and contented, bathed, drank, dozed in front of the fire and read a detective story, an old green three-layer Penguin that he had found in the lounge bookshelf, left behind by some previous visitor. He even watched television. It was a day plucked out of time, it belonged to him alone, unshared with Sir Jacob or the others, the mysterious *Them*. He hoped that it would not be long before he was back in the Middle East. Thinking of the Middle East and of his job reminded him of Petros and he bought a postcard at the desk to send to him. He wondered whether it would arrive after he did. The day slipped by uneventful, relaxing, wholly enjoyable. By its end he felt much better, he even looked forward to Monday.

He caught the first ferry Monday morning – the journey was a beautiful one, Duart Castle on the right, the flag flying showing that its owner was in residence, gulls swooped and circled the ship – in the galley he had a bacon roll and a cup of tea. On deck it was cold, the wind bit into his legs and the small of his back. He decided that he would get out of Oban as soon as possible, there was a Glasgow train, then when he got to Dalmally or Crianlarich he could change and wait, it would be safer not to stay either at Oban or Glasgow.

At the station he bought a couple of papers before catching the train. Before the senseless and short-sighted Beeching massacre the train had had a buffet car and in the season an observation car as well. Beeching had abolished these and closed down stations on the line like Loch Awe, actions that had hastened the coach and car explosion.

He got off at Crianlarich, a station with more certificates for excellence than any other on that line, checked that his sleeper was booked and left his rucksack in the office. After that he took a short walk before dusk fell, then tea in the restaurant. He sat in front of the lounge fire doing the crossword puzzle. Time passed very slowly. From tea he went to the hotel bar and drank until it was time for the train.

At last it was time for the train: it came in on time, the first-class sleepers were not full, a Liberal MP on his way to Westminster, a new Lord with an unfamiliar name, a Lt Col. Snelling MC and a couple of other names. The attendant took his ticket and asked when he wanted his morning tea.

'Six, please, I always wake early.'

'There's a mini-buffet down the train, sir, you can get a drink and sandwich there – it comes off at Glasgow.'

He walked down and found the car with the Urn. A number of passengers surrounded it, including an attractive young man in a dark sweater and tight, pale-blue jeans.

He bought a drink and a sandwich – the young man was drinking lager from the can. The train braked suddenly and they were flung together, some of the beer spilt.

'I say, I am sorry.'

'That's all right.' He mopped a damp spot.

'You going far?'

'Yes, to London, are you?'

'London too.'

They chatted for some minutes – Michael thought of Petros; it had been a long time. The beer finished, they began to walk back to their compartments.

'Would you like a whisky, I've some in my sleeper?'

'I don't mind, thanks.'

'Right, come along.'

When the attendant took Michael his tea next morning he found the body, naked, a knife sticking from the ribs, hands and feet tied, a handkerchief in his mouth – he kept his head, noticing that blood still seemed to be oozing from the edges of the wound. He remembered that the Colonel was in the RAMC. He banged on the door.

'Sir, sir, please, sir.'

'Eh, yes, what's the matter?'

The Colonel, indeed an army doctor, was awake, reading. The attendant explained what had happened.

'Right, just wait a minute,' he pulled on his trousers, grasped his bag and followed the man to the sleeper.

'Yes, he's still alive. Here, help me.'

Some minutes later after he had untied and ungagged the unconscious Michael he turned to the attendant.

'How much longer to Euston?'

'Fifteen minutes, sir.'

'Good, I shan't take the knife out for it would only start the wound bleeding – but luckily it seems to have missed both heart and lungs, there's a good chance if we can get him to hospital quickly: now, go and find the guard and bring some more blankets. He must be kept warm.'

Michael's pulse was steady: the train slid into Euston; within a very short time the ambulance had arrived and the police too. The journey was over.

CHAPTER TEN

The Mugging of Andrew

'A time for sowing'

THERE have been some noble and memorable descriptions of Kenya. I still consider Karen Blixen's *Out of Africa* to be one of the world's Golden Books. To read it is to experience again the sights and sounds and perhaps above all to savour the smells of early morning, when often a blue mist lies over the land and the air is cold and tastes of Africa, an indescribable but easily recognizable taste to those who have experienced it. There is a quietness but not that of the cloister; rather it is a stillness punctuated by small sounds, birds chattering in the trees, the crackle of sticks being broken by the women making fires, sounds that carry for miles across the plains, the call of a beast in pain or on heat – a mosaic of noises. The enjoyment of such experiences is enormously pleasurable. It may be that as a race we are affected by nostalgia, today's distress and frustrations when they become yesterday's are smoothed or transfigured or quite simply forgotten.

It was a day or two after my arrival. Father's head boy, except that this dangerous and emotive word 'boy' had been replaced by that of 'steward', brought me a tray of morning tea. It was six o'clock.

'*Jambo, Bwana.*'

'*Jambo,* Ali, *asante sana,*' then I gave up, it was too early to try to remember my best kitchen Swahili.

'Ali.'

'Yes, *Bwana*.'

'I think that I should like to ride this morning, is there a horse for me?'

'Yes, *Bwana*.'

'Now?'

'I will tell the syce, he will make one ready.'

'I have no clothes.'

'Yes, *Bwana*, from your last visit.'

I had forgotten, but when I had last visited my father I had left behind some of my clothes. These Ali had washed and ironed and put away, carefully protected from white ants and moths.

By the time that I had drunk my tea, washed and dressed in the moth-ball-smelling riding breeches, the syce had saddled a horse and brought it round to the front of the house. My father appeared in his dressing-gown, drinking tea from a pint-sized mug.

'Morning, Adam.'

'Good morning, Dad.'

'I'm glad you've decided to ride, horses need exercise, the syce will go with you, don't y'know?'

'Really?'

'Yes, a bit unsettled at the moment, not too bad but it is better not to go too far alone – I'd rather you didn't.'

'Right, that's no problem.' I walked from the verandah to where the syce was holding two horses.

My father called out: 'Elimu, let my son have Karen, you take Amani,' then to me: 'Adam, she should give you no trouble but don't use a whip, treat her with great gentleness.'

The blue mist covered the land, it lay in whorls like smoke in a bar, but smoke without its acrid tobacco taste and smell.

Although I remembered the farm and the surrounding countryside quite well I decided to let the syce lead, 'Elimu, you go first, you know where we can go.'

He grinned, 'OK, *Bwana*,' he said, and trotted ahead down the drive to the main farm road. Soon we were in open country. It was this Kenya that had won the hearts of the early settlers and embedded itself in their affections; and it was this Kenya that kept so many of their descendants tied to the country even though they were little better than second-class citizens. On mornings such as this, so peaceful and seemingly eternal, they could dream of the easy days of Empire, days when the laws seemed few and life, if sometimes difficult when the banks were pressing, was free and the sun was always shining. Forgotten were the long droughts, the locust swarms, the soldier ants, and the sudden storms when the heavens opened and floods swept away crops and cattle and topsoil. These calamities were bearable, became indeed bar-room stories, folk memories, because there was always hope; eternal optimism gilded the thinking and the purposes of these men and women. Happy Valley excesses were not the norm, they shocked, absorbed, delighted, gave a certain extra piquancy to days when the price of pyrethrum and the arrival of the Royal Mail ship were the subject of conversations.

This day when Elimu the syce and I rode in the morning silence was one of those marvellous days, and the troubles in England seemed indeed a long way away. They dwindled, faded like the Cheshire cat, but the image of Rory remained strong and immediate. I wished that I could have brought him with me, have shown him this tremendous country.

'*Bwana*, see,' Elimu pointed forward towards a place above which vultures were swirling and gathering. A kill, an imminent death, one or the other. I shuddered in anticipation. Perhaps there were lion there or cheetah. I dug my heels in, urging my horse forward.

'No, *Bwana*, no, no gun, *Bwana mkubwa* would not like.'

Damn, Elimu was right, if there were only one lion it would not much matter, but a pride, then there was the potential for trouble, and there would be hyaena there, that most vicious killer of all. I had once watched a pack of hyaena pull down and kill a great bull buffalo at a water hole, a horrific sight which lacked the speed and artistry of the kill of a cheetah or a lion. I had longed then for a gun with which to put the beast out of his agony.

We turned back, I, reluctantly, to the farm, cantering across the plains, the horses eager to get home – a Tommie buck leapt away from a group of grazing does and the harem bounded away.

I decided to tell my father why I had come, so at breakfast, after a shower, I explained why I had come out so suddenly. He had listened intently, only occasionally asking a question. When I finished, 'What do you want?' he had asked. 'How can that woman help you?'

'When I met her yesterday at the pool with that man Major Hall I did establish some kind of rapport. We have agreed to meet again. I did not much care for her, too lacquered for my liking – burnished and polished (I misquoted) by sun lamps and lotion.'

'Do you think she knows anything?'

'I don't know Dad, that's one of the things that I must find out, but I must talk to her, I must find out who she meets, what she does – wait, watch and search.'

'Well, what do you intend to do now?'

'I don't know, I'm a bit lost. I imagine, no I know that I must get nearer to this woman – Sir Jacob, Dad, is so sure that she is involved in buying or moving the drugs.'

My father was silent.'

'What do you suggest, Dad?'

He pulled at his left ear and gazed out at the garden where the shamba boy was standing waiting for instructions.

'Today, do nothing, you have to establish in her mind that you really are on holiday, with no purpose but to see me and enjoy yourself. Go to the hotel this morning, she may be there, have a swim, take Andrew with you, I'll join you at lunch.' It seemed excellent advice. My father wandered off into the garden and began talking with the shamba boy – the boy gesticulated, I could not hear what was being said, both seemed happy. Ali came and began to clear away.

'Ali.'

'*Bwana.*'

'Have you seen my brother anywhere?'

'Yes, *Bwana*, he's gone out.'

'Where?'

'To the duka – he took the small car.'

'Thank you, Ali.'

I began to think about Rory. What, I wondered, was he doing, was he all right? Was his 'minder' replacing me in his affections – he was, after all, much nearer in age to Rory and could match his energy. Perhaps I should ring. But I must not fuss. I went into the garden where my father had finished his discussions.

'Dad.'

'Yes, Adam.'

'What do you really think about all this, am I mad?' Why should I care what he thought? It was a strange development that now after years of partial neglect I should genuinely seek my father's advice. We had always had a comfortable relationship based, certainly latterly, on a mutual respect and affection, but on my side at least I had never until this visit felt close to him. It had been reassuring to know that he was there if I wanted him – even though there were thousands of miles between us – and he had shown pleasure in seeing me on my visits, but I had never sought his advice on anything of importance, or discussed decisions with him. My decisions had been my own. Perhaps it was because of Rory and my surrogate fatherhood that now I wanted to exploit, if that is really the right word, our relationship. I wanted, indeed, his approbation.

He thought for a moment before answering, cutting off a falling rose with the knife he always carried.

'Adam, you know I've never tried to interfere with what you were doing, perhaps I've neglected you, but you have known that I was here and that if you wanted a home you had one.'

'Yes, Dad.'

'I haven't agreed with much of what you have done in the past, some of your friends I have found tiresome and rather silly – those youngsters from the theatre whom you used to run around with.'

He had never really liked Hélène – now I seldom thought of her, there were no scars. What a silly notion, of course I thought of her. I remembered the good times, it was the memory of the bad that had faded.

'Yes, Dad.'

'However,' he went on, 'I think that what you are now doing is right, really rather splendid, and I shall do all I can to help, but what do you want me to do? Have you a plan? Have I a role?'

'No, I've nothing to go on yet.'

The small car drew up and Andrew got out.

'Hi, Adam.' He came over and joined us.

'Andrew, take him to the hotel for a swim, introduce him to some of the new neighbours.'

'Righto, Dad, will do.'

My father turned away and walked into the house.

'Sorry, Adam, was I interrupting.'

'No, Andrew, it's all right. We'd finished – let's go.'

We collected our trunks and towels and I chose a couple of green Penguins to read.

An hour or so later we were lying on mattresses by the hotel pool. Andrew edged his nearer to mine. He turned and leant on one elbow.

'Adam, I want to come to England. There's no future here for me.'

'What do you want to do? Art?'

Andrew paused, he seemed in some doubt about what to say.

'Yes, I want to go to Art School – I love drawing and design. I'd like to be a designer.'

'Well, why not?'

'Dad.'

'Dad?'

'Yes, if I go I'll leave him on his own, there is no one to look after him.'

'Do you think that he needs someone?'

'Yes I do, he gets terribly lonely. I notice it in the evening. When I was still at school he was pretty miserable during term time – Ali told me so – he tried to hide it, he hated my going back after the holidays much more than I did.'

'Do you have to go?'

'Yes, there is no future for me here; honestly there isn't. I'll never get a top job, I'm white, we'll always be strangers here even if I married a local girl. I am a second-class citizen. I could be deported tomorrow at the whim of some minister. Adam, I want to be my own master, to be able to shout and complain when I want to. It's all right for Dad and his generation, and for the very rich who can and do fly to England for the races. Dad's settled, he's servants and the sun, he really is OK, he only wants to sit and watch the garden grow, his ambition is spent.'

'But do you think he needs someone here, with him all the time?'

'I don't know.'

'How old are you now, nineteen?'

'Yes.'

'What do you want me to do, speak to Dad?'

'Will you?'

'Of course I will – but tell me, Andrew, there's nothing else bothering you, some other reason you want to get away?'

'No,' he shut up like a clam and rolled over on to his back. 'No there's nothing else, nothing.'

'OK, OK, there's nothing else. I'll speak to Dad as soon as a good opportunity arises.'

'Thanks, Adam.' He put out his hand and touched my arm, 'thanks.'

The sun beat down – I rubbed in some more oil. At this height, although it seemed reasonably cool, the sun was strong and burnt the unwary; luckily I soon brown.

'Here let me do that, turn over.'

I turned on my stomach and Andrew began to rub oil into my shoulders.

'I'm sorry,' he said, 'there is another reason.'

'Uhum.'

'I'm frightened.'

'Frightened?' I turned over to look at him. 'Frightened, what on earth do you mean?'

'I'll tell you, but please first you must promise not to tell Dad, do you promise?'

'How can I make such a promise? It would be unfair, you must trust me and I promise that I won't let you down. If I do tell Dad anything it will only be if it really is essential for him to know – trust my judgement, please.'

'Oh, all right: yes, I'm in trouble, I need help.'

'Yes?'

He rubbed my back with fierce determination.

'Hey, it's my back – you're hurting.'

He laughed, 'Sorry, I wasn't thinking.'

Then the silence again. Birds circled overhead, and in the trees weavers were busy building their nests. In the distance I heard a car start and drive away. Someone in the hotel called out, 'Abdullah, Ab-dull-ah, come here please, Ab-dull-ah.'

Andrew began, hesitantly at first then with more confidence.

'Some weeks ago I went to a party, someone doped my drink, I was stoned, absolutely – they took photographs.'

'Photographs, have you seen them?'

'Yes.'

'And . . .?'

'They're awful, me and a black girl and . . .' he paused '. . . and a black boy – Adam they're awful.'

I could tell from the movement of his hands on my back how agitated he was.

'Steady on, you'll have my skin off.'

'Sorry' he laughed, 'I'm always saying sorry.'

'Have they asked you for money?'

'No, nothing, he just showed me the prints and said that we'd have a talk sometime.'

'Who was it?' Silence. 'For heaven's sake, Andrew, if you've told me so much you can't not tell me who it is. How can I help you if I don't know?'

More silence.

'Major Hall,' a whisper only.

'What!' I leapt up, sending the bottle of oil spinning out of his hand.

'Hey.'

'Andrew,' I sat down on his mattress, 'Andrew, is this true, you're not telling me a story are you?'

'No, of course not, do you think that I would joke about something like this?'

'I don't think so. I will help, but you must give me time to think. I've got to telephone. You wait here. I'll be back.'

I pulled on my trousers, buttoned up my shirt and hurried to the buggy. I could hardly wait, here was the break for which I had been looking.

At the farm I telephoned London. Infuriatingly it took some time to get through.

'Sir Jacob, please.'

'He's not here, he's at luncheon.'

'Get him, please, I must speak to him.'

'He's lunching with the Minister.'

'It's urgent, really, please give him a message, please. He'll be grateful, I promise.'

'All right I'll tell him – *now*, it's a promise, put the receiver down.' I paced up and down in a passion of impatience.

Seven minutes later the telephone bell rang. I picked up the receiver.

'Adam.'

'Sir.'

'It had better be good.'

'I've a lead, I must have all the information you have on a Major David Hall.'

I told him briefly what I had discovered.

'Good, good, we'll ring you back, stay by the 'phone, don't leave it – understood?'

'Understood, sir.'

'Good, we'll talk later.'

'Ali, Ali,' I shouted, 'where is my father?'

Ali appeared in the hall. 'He's gone into town, *Bwana*, he said he was going to see a man about some sheep.'

'Damn.'

'Yes, *Bwana*.'

'Ali, please could you take the buggy down to the pool. I had to leave Andrew there. Tell him please that I have to wait here for a telephone call, bring him back with you.'

'Yes, *Bwana*.'

Ali had been with my father for years, several years before Andrew was born – he had been responsible for Andrew's early upbringing, beating him when he was disobedient, comforting him when he fell over and hurt himself. He still treated Andrew as a naughty schoolboy.

'*Bwana?*'

'Yes.'

'*Bwana*, what is the trouble?' The old man came and stood by me.

'Ali, there is trouble, bad trouble and some of it concerns Andrew, we have to be careful.'

Ali shook his head. 'I'll go now,' he said and was gone.

The telephone bell rang some minutes later.

'We have the information; your friend has a most interesting dossier. An unsavoury record. Cashiered from the army – embezzled mess funds; involved in the running of a shady club in the early sixties, smelled of blackmail, left England soon after the club was closed. In court for assault but acquitted for lack of evidence.'

'Any drug connection?'

'No evidence so far, but the investigation continues. Adam?'

'Yes, sir.'

'Adam, I shall get in touch with an old friend in Nairobi, he is attached to the Ministry of the Interior, he will give you all the help you need. His name is Captain Joab arap Kirui. I'll warn him that you will be getting in touch with him, and Adam . . .'

'Yes, sir?'

'Be careful, these people have already killed: there is big money involved.'

'Right you are sir.'

'Good – keep in touch.' He rang off.

There were several courses of action open to me. One was to go and see Major Hall, confront him and demand the return of the photographs and negatives. But there would probably be prints elsewhere and I had no means of forcing Hall to hand them over. When I am unsettled and need to think I walk up and down. Now I paced the verandah trying to work out how best to deal with the situation, how to accomplish my mission and how to extricate my brother from his troubles. Not easy at all.

The buggy returned, my brother came to the verandah.

'I've seen him.'

'Who – Hall?'

'Yes.'

'What did he say, what does he want?'

'He's invited us, both of us, to a party, he particularly wants you to go. I hedged a bit saying that I'd try to persuade you but that I wasn't sure what you were doing.'

'Good, that was right.'

'I need a beer,' Andrew disappeared to the kitchen.

A possible solution suggested itself to me. At the last moment I would go down with a funny tummy; a perfectly valid excuse for a visitor, especially in this heat. I wanted to work out a coherent plan, no false starts.

Luckily my father had decided that he would stay the night of Major Hall's party in Nairobi at the Muthaiga Club, he had a morning appointment and he preferred to go to it fresh rather than after a dusty, bumpy car ride. He would have dinner with an old friend who lived in Ngong and who would come over to the Club for the occasion. Andrew had telephoned Hall to thank him on my behalf and to tell him that I hoped to be at the party. Andrew and I were sitting talking after tea.

'Look,' I said, 'this is what I think you should do, what I want you to do. Firstly don't drink any of the drinks given to you, only those you help yourself to – the same with food, don't take what is offered, eat only the food you choose; secondly pretend to get a little drunk, but leave early; and lastly watch Mrs Moore and the Major. Is that clear?'

'Yes, I think so, anything else?'

'Well, I am not really ready yet but if you could let drop at the party, so that the Major hears, that you're planning to leave with me when my stay is over it might be productive: I want to force them to take action. Do you mind?'

'No: will it be dangerous?'

'I don't think so – no, that's wrong. It may well be dangerous. You have to be very careful and not over-react, don't be over-confident.'

'What do you think will happen?'

THE SCENT OF POPPIES

'I don't know, I am not sure, probably they'll try to pressurize you to stay: they may even try to use physical force, but I doubt it. Blackmail is more their line – remember, other people like you will be there and if they see that your rebellion is successful, unchallenged, they may be tempted themselves to resist Hall's demands – that is a challenge Hall cannot risk. Fear is his main weapon.' I stood up.

'Croquet?'

'OK.'

We played and as usual Andrew won, both games. Then it was time for him to dress. I wrote a short note for him to take, excusing myself on account of an 'internal upset'. I wandered into the kitchen.

'Ali,' I said, I don't want much tonight: soup and an omelette will be enough.'

'*Ndio, Bwana.*'

Darkness had fallen. Andrew came out into the hall neatly suited, hair plastered down, face shining – a picture of triumphant youth.

'Not evening dress!'

'No, by special request.'

It is a strange comment that here in the tropics in one of the deserted, abandoned provinces of Empire, dressing for dinner was more common than in Imperial Rome itself.

'Be careful, Andrew, please.'

'Right you are!' He smiled somewhat wanly, then he was gone. I went early to bed.

I was woken by the sound of banging doors, dogs barking, and the servants shouting. Ali appeared at the door.

'*Bwana, Bwana*, come quickly. Andrew . . .'

I leapt naked out of bed, put on a pair of shorts and ran into the hall. Andrew was slouched in a chair, blood dribbling down his face from a wound in his head, his clothes torn and filthy, his mouth bruised and bleeding. Suddenly he retched and was sick all over the floor. The place reeked of alcohol.

'Andrew . . . Ali, Ali, ring for the doctor.'

'No.' Andrew gesticulated wildly and tried to get up. He managed with difficulty to speak, the words slurred and indistinct. 'No, please, no doctor.'

'Ali, hot water, towels, tea, brandy, quick.'

Ali had regained his composure; he was once more in charge – towels and a basin of hot water appeared, gently I wiped some of the blood and vomit from poor Andrew's battered face. I chattered all the time, small talk, seeking to reassure him and to keep my concern and disgust hidden. Keep calm, I must keep calm.

'Andrew, can you talk, what happened?'

'There, there was a row; they beat me up – ouch that hurt.'

'Sorry.'

'God I feel awful.'

'Can you stand?'

'I think so.' He held my arm. I supported him on one side and Ali on the other. We got him groaning and moaning to my bathroom.

'Sit down.' The kitchen boy appeared with a tray of tea.

'Ali, put some brandy in the tea and plenty of sugar.'

'Yes, *Bwana*.'

'Here, Andrew, try to drink some of this.' He swallowed and choked. We stripped him down to his briefs and I began to clean him up. The cut in his head was luckily not so deep as I feared at first although blood was still seeping from it.

'This'll hurt,' I said as I dabbed the cuts with antiseptic. Andrew shivered; his body was badly bruised and there were cuts and abrasions on his thighs and legs where he had been kicked. I was worried by the shivering.

'I still think you should see a doctor.'

'No, no,' his voice took on a panicky pitch. 'Please, Adam, I don't want him, he fusses.'

'*Bwana*.'

'Yes, Ali.'

'*Bwana*, there is Doctor Elsie.'

'Ali, you're brilliant. Of course, Doctor Elsie's the answer – you wouldn't mind her would you Andrew?'

'No.'

Dr Elsie McLaren was a retired doctor living on the farm next to my father's – she grew vegetables, watched birds, and fished; she was an old family friend and had known Andrew all his life. I dialled her number. The bell rang loudly at the other end. It was some time before she answered.

'101, Elsie McLaren.' Her voice was heavy with sleep.

'Elsie, it's Adam Masson here. I'm sorry to disturb you but we're in trouble, Andrew's been beaten up and I think he should see a doctor, can you help?'

'How bad is he?'

'Not too bad, he can stand but he's wobbly and he can't stop shivering. We'll send Ali for you.'

'Yes, of course I'll come. I'll be ready by the time Ali gets here.'

I sighed with relief. 'You heard that, Ali, Dr Elsie will come, please take the buggy and go and pick her up.'

Ali was delighted, pleased with the development.

'*Bwana*, make Andrew drink more tea.'

Andrew was still shivering.

'Would you like a bath?'

'Yes, please: they kicked me in the balls.'

'Ugh,' I pulled off his briefs and helped him into the bath. He lay in the water, but would not let go of my hand. He drank the tea with my help.

'Moshi, Moshi,' I called. Moshi was the kitchen boy.

'*Ndio, Bwana.*'

Moshi, please make us some more tea.'

'OK, *Bwana.*'

I let some more hot water into the bath. The tea soon came – and not long after, Dr Elsie. Andrew was out of the bath, I was drying him, he clutched the towel to cover himself with.

'Tch, boy, I've seen more men naked than you ever have, and as for you, have you forgotten the times I've bathed you? Don't be silly.'

Dr Elsie examined Andrew very carefully. Her hands were still strong and beautiful (she wore gloves when gardening) and they moved over Andrew's body gently probing.

'Does that hurt? No, good and that?'

'Aaah.'

'That hurts does it?'

'Yes.'

At last: 'Well, there's nothing broken and you don't need stitches, that cut is not deep and should heal without too much bother, but you are quite badly bruised and I am afraid that you may pass blood for a day or two, but don't worry, after two or three days that'll clear up but you're going to be sore and stiff and uncomfortable. Drink a lot of water or tea but no more alcohol.' She turned to me.

'Adam, you're to see that he has plenty of rest; what you tell your father is your business not mine, but I think you'll have to think of a convincing story.' On her way out to the buggy I asked her whether Andrew really was not too badly damaged. 'Yes he's mostly bruised and superficially cut, but he will certainly be very sore and he is

THE MUGGING OF ANDREW

obviously badly shaken. I've some sleeping pills here, strong ones, give him two now and he'll sleep for hours – and two later on, and do remember no alcohol. I'll look in tomorrow – at least it's today now, in the late afternoon to see how he is.'

'Thank you for coming and for not asking questions.'

She patted my arm. 'Don't worry, Adam, he'll be all right, he is very fit, you know.'

Ali drove her home.

I went into the kitchen and collected some hot milk. Andrew was half sitting up and half slouched in a chair in my room. He looked scared.

'Adam, please, don't leave me.'

He sounded pretty desperate. I looked at him, and saw not a young man but a badly frightened small boy.

'I won't,' I answered. 'I'll tell you what I'll do, I'll get Ali to bring another bed in here, then you'll be safe.'

I'd forgotten for the moment that Ali had gone with Dr Elsie so instead I went into the spare room and took a camp bed from the cupboard and brought it into mine.

'You take my bed, come on I'll help you.' He winced a little as he hobbled to my bed. He got in and I gave him the two tablets and the hot milk. He held my hand. 'Don't leave me, Adam, please.'

He sounded as though he would panic if I left so I sat on the edge of the bed and held his hand.

'You won't leave me, promise, please.'

'No I won't, I promise, but let me go and get myself a drink.'

'All right.'

I went and made myself a drink. Ali soon returned from taking Dr Elsie back to her farm. He held a scarf in his hand.

'*Bwana*,' he said, 'this was in the front seat of the car.'

He gave me the scarf – it was green and gold, silk.

'Thank you, Ali,' I said, 'this may be useful.' I took it and put it in the bureau drawer.

'Now, Ali, please, will you make up the camp bed for me, I'm going to sleep in the room with Andrew.'

Andrew gripped my hand; luckily it was not long before he fell asleep, the tablets were strong and worked quickly.

It took me a long time to get back to sleep, then suddenly it was dawn. Andrew slept on.

I got up and went to the kitchen to make myself a cup of tea. Ali was already there.

'What happened, *Bwana*?' he asked.

'Ali, I don't know but I am determined to find out.'

I did not dare to ring London from the house; I feared that the line might now be tapped. But there was one number I could ring and I did; at eight, I rang Major Hall. When I got through to the house his servant took a little time to fetch him.

'Hello, hello,' I said. 'Oh, Major, I am sorry to disturb you so early but my brother asked me to, he was most anxious that I should get in touch and apologise for his behaviour last night. He must have had far too much to drink and did not know what he was doing or saying.'

'My dear chap it was nothing, a little local difficulty, what – and are you better?'

Was I better? Then I remembered – 'Oh yes, much, thank you, I'm nearly settled now, back to normal, the worst is over.'

'But don't worry about Andrew, old boy, he was a little rowdy, but no damage done, tell him not to worry – all is forgiven.'

'That's very decent of you, thank you. I'm sure my father would want to thank you too.' I paused,

'Major . . .'

'Yes.'

'Major, do you happen to know who drove Andrew back here, he couldn't have driven himself? I should like to thank whoever it was.'

'No, I'm sorry, oh wait a minute, of course I know, it was Eileen Moore, she was the good Samaritan.'

'How did she get back?'

'Oh, her driver followed her, I gather.'

'Thank you again, Major, and once more, Andrew is most contrite, his behaviour was disgraceful, I hope to see you soon.'

I must telephone Nairobi and London, what should I do? Then I remembered Dr Elsie. I would go there.

'Ali, Ali, I'm just going over to Amani Cottage to see Dr Elsie – when Andrew wakes up keep him in bed, but let him have what he wants for breakfast, it will do him good to eat.'

'*Ndio, Bwana.*'

'But, Ali, no alcohol, absolutely no alcohol.'

I drove over to Elsie's. She was pottering in the garden, secateurs in her hand.

'Hullo, Adam.'

'Morning, Doctor.'

'How's Andrew this morning?'

'Still asleep when I left, I gave him a couple of those sleeping tablets.'

'Excellent, come and have a cup of coffee.'

We sat on the verandah watching the sunbirds at the flowering creepers; Elsie looked hard at me.

'Adam, do you know what actually happened?'

'No, honestly I don't know; I can guess but it is only a guess; please don't ask me yet.'

'Very well.'

'Elsie, please may I use your telephone? I think our one may be tapped.'

'Of course.'

I went inside into the study, the old consulting room. I dialled the number that Sir Jacob had given me.

It was some time before the phone was answered.

'Hullo, good morning, may I help you?'

'Yes please, I should like to speak to Captain arap Kirui.'

'Who is speaking, sir?'

'My name,' I said, 'is Adam Masson.'

Almost immediately a voice said, 'Joab arap Kirui here, Mr Masson: how can I help you?'

'Sir,' I said, 'Sir Jacob told me that I should get in touch with you if there was any trouble, and there is.'

I told him briefly what had happened, I kept the story of the photographs to myself, I did not trust the telephone.

'I think I ought to come and see you: could I come this afternoon?'

'Yes, any time after 2.30, do you know where to come?'

'No.'

'I'm on the third floor of Oxbridge House, Room 314 – OK?'

'Yes, sir, I'll be there.'

'Good,' the receiver was put down.

'Elsie, I'll get back now, thank you for the coffee.'

'Very well, Adam, tell Andrew that I'll be over nearer lunchtime.'

I drove back to the farm. Ali was waiting for me, he had heard the car.

'Ali.'

'Yes, *Bwana*.'

'Is Andrew awake yet?'

'Yes, *Bwana*, he's had tea and some orange juice.'
'Good.'
I went into my room, Andrew was sitting up in bed drinking his tea: he looked a mess – a piece of Elastoplast over the cut on his forehead, two purple bloodshot eyes, swollen lips and where his naked body showed above the sheets, purple and yellow bruises on his arms and shoulders.
'Morning.'
He tried to grin. 'Morning, Adam, how do I look?'
'Bloody awful, but don't worry, it will pass, how do you feel?'
'Pretty grim actually, and rather muzzy.'
'Have you pee'd yet?'
'Yes, that was terrible, really terrible. I'm so sore, I'm still swollen.'
'I think that you'd better stay in bed, but have a bath, Elsie should be here before lunch.
I turned on the bath and Andrew stumbled out of bed.
Earlier I had telephoned Muthaiga and spoken to my father. I had told him what appeared to have happened and I assured him that Andrew was in no danger and that Elsie was looking after him. If anyone was listening they would have heard the 'official' story.
I decided that I ought to begin making arrangements for Andrew's visit to England. I went back into the bathroom where Andrew was soaking in a steaming bath.
'Andrew, old chap I'm going to Nairobi to get your ticket to London – is your passport up to date?'
'Yes, no problem there.'
'What is it – British or Kenyan?'
'British.'
'Good that makes it easier.' Andrew had been born in London although most of his life had been spent in Kenya.
'You'll be OK until Dad gets back, I won't be too long either. Don't worry, Ali's here and I am sure nothing will happen, they'll want you to reflect, to sweat, and to worry.'
I went to get ready. The green and gold scarf intrigued me. It should not be too difficult to prove that it was Mrs Moore's; after all, the Major had admitted that it was she who had brought Andrew home, there was no secret about her action. I changed into a tropical suit – Nairobi visiting clothes – for if I were to call on Sir Jacob's friend I would have to look respectable; shorts and Aertex shirt were definitely not suitable for such an occasion. It was shortly after eleven

and I was ready to go. I looked into Andrew's room. He was once more fast asleep, looking now much more peaceful, gently snoring. He looked, as indeed he was, an overgrown small boy. I heard a car draw up outside, the dogs barked, I went out. Mrs Moore was getting out of the blue Volvo, a uniformed driver holding the door for her – cool, smiling, composed, a studied look of compassion on her face. She advanced towards me.

'Good morning.'

'Good morning,' she answered, 'I've called to see how your brother Andrew is. You know I brought him back here last night.'

'Come in, may I offer you a drink?'

'No thank you, it is a little early for me, but I would love a cup of coffee, would that be possible?'

'Of course; Ali.'

Ali, who had been standing in the doorway, went off to the kitchen.

'I hope,' I said, 'that Andrew did not cause too much trouble, he seems to have been pretty drunk.'

'No, he was quite docile,' she said. 'My driver and I brought him home, we put him in the back of the buggy, I drove and Mbotha followed in my car.'

'What actually happened? He does not seem to remember anything very clearly.'

'What has he said?'

'Nothing, he was too confused and incoherent last night, and too drunk, and this morning he is still asleep.'

'That's good, he will probably be much better when he wakes up – after a good rest.'

'But what did Andrew do, do you know?'

'No I don't, he made a good deal of noise and was rather offensive in a childish way, then disappeared for a time, he must have had a bad fight for when I found him he was on his back on David's verandah and one of the servants was trying to rouse him, he was out to the world.'

'Do you know who was fighting with him?'

'No that's the strange thing, his injuries must have been caused by someone, but none of the other guests seems to have been involved, the servants refuse to say anything, it must have been a gatecrasher.'

She drank her coffee which Ali had brought. I remembered the scarf and went over to the drawer of the writing desk and took it out.

'I think you must have left your scarf in the buggy; it is yours isn't it?' I showed her the scarf.

'Yes, it is, I wondered where I had lost it, thank you so much, it is a favourite of mine.'

She put down her coffee cup and slowly stood up, brushing down her skirt. 'I really must go now.'

'It was so good of you to call,' I said. 'I know my father would want to thank you for bringing Andrew back safely.'

'Not at all, it was nothing. You will come over one day won't you?'

'I'd love to do that: may I telephone tomorrow?'

'Of course.'

The dialogue was stilted: it was as though we were characters in some radio play. Did he know more than he said? Did she guess that he knew what had really happened? Had Andrew talked or was he too frightened? Had the message got through: co-operate? It was fascinating but probably dangerous, Andrew and I would have to be careful. I walked with her to the car, her driver leapt to his feet and opened the door.

'I'm driving to Nairobi in half an hour or so,' I said, 'perhaps we shall meet, will you go to Muthaiga?'

'No,' she answered, 'not today, today some old Asian friends of my husband's have asked me to luncheon. Afterwards I have to go to the travel agents to see about the possibility of going on to Sri Lanka.'

'A pity, we might have met for tea.'

She smiled and held out her hand. 'Thank you so much for the coffee – and for the scarf.'

'Not at all, thank you for helping Andrew last night.'

'Goodbye.'

The car disappeared down the drive. Ali was at my shoulder. He shook his head. 'Not one of my memsahibs,' he said, 'not one of the old ones like Dr Elsie.'

'No she isn't: now I must be off too: Ali, look after Andrew, don't let him get up or go out.'

'No *Bwana*' Ali smiled. 'I'll tell him I'll beat him as I used to when he was disobedient.'

'Well done, Ali.'

CHAPTER ELEVEN

London Interlude

'Yet there is something in it, tricks and all.'

SOON after I had departed for Kenya in pursuit of Mrs Moore Sir Jacob had started planning the operation that was to close down the drug ring. He had many problems to solve in distinguishing the tributaries that constituted the main river: the first was that presented by the suppliers, by the people in parts of Asia who were growing and supplying the drugs to Kenya; the second by the Kenya connection, the dhow owners, the transporters of the drugs to Great Britain; the third by the receivers in Britain to whom the drugs were sent; the fourth the distributors who sold the drugs in the streets and schools; and lastly the customers, the clients who bought and used the drugs.

Starting backwards and using the information that Michael McNab had gathered in Tiree he could close down many of the distributors on the list without too much trouble.

'Look, Minister,' he said, 'let me show you a simple diagram,' and he placed a sheet of paper before the formidable grey-haired woman who was the Minister theoretically in charge of the Department. The diagram, he later showed it to me, was simple enough but it did help to distinguish the different strands of the problem.

'It looks like a blueprint for a mobile.'

Sir Jacob ignored the comment. 'I cannot do anything about the first part, the foreign government concerned would have to act, that's your responsibility, madam.'

'Yes,' the Minister said, 'but you are aware, Sir Jacob, as well as I am that it is almost impossible to persuade these governments to do anything, they're so riddled with inefficiency and personal corruption. They are not decision-makers. And,' she added, 'the growers do have large sums of money at their disposal, so indeed do the exporters.'

'You could perhaps bring pressure, Minister, threaten to cancel loans, to withhold aid.'

'No, it never works, we have tried in other circumstances, there is no expert infrastructure and the will power is lacking.'

Sir Jacob looked out of the window, a traffic warden was writing out tickets.

'We can close down the Kenya end, Minister: the man in charge is an old friend, he served here for a time, he has the information on which he can act, he is an excellent man, decisive.'

'What will he do?'

'Well he can make it difficult but not impossible for the dhows, the coast is too long to man completely and he has not enough men. But he can destroy the local organization. The expatriates will be expelled, the local people prosecuted, the exporting companies wound up.'

'That is good, is it not?'

'Yes, Minister it is, but it would not be for long, either through Kenya or from elsewhere drugs would start moving again. The only real answer is to destroy the crops in the fields – and who will do that?'

' – and here?'

'Here, well we know where the drugs are landed and we know where they go and we know how they are distributed – this we could deal with now, but whether we can catch the big fish is not clear, we have not enough evidence.'

'Do you know who the big fish is?'

'I'm not sure, I've a pretty good idea, but I'm not really sure – I don't want to act yet. I need more time.'

'Have we the time, Sir Jacob?'

'Well, it is difficult to know, it's a matter of choice. What is the more important – to catch the leader and let some of the smaller men escape or to close the operation down now?'

'Well, Sir Jacob, for the moment it is your choice, but before long it may be mine, especially if there is a press leak.'

The Minister got up from her chair and smoothed down her skirt

— she was a person of considerable presence, belonging perhaps rather to the pre-war category of women MPs than to that of the brash and brassy Thatcher type. Sir Jacob had great respect for her judgement.

'I really must go now, there is a meeting I am obliged to attend: but do please keep me up to date with what happens.'

'Thank you, Minister.'

Sir Jacob's secretary, the admirable Mavis, appeared at the door.

'The Minister's car is ready, Sir Jacob.'

'Thank you, Mavis.'

When the Minister had gone Sir Jacob sat, silent, deep in thought, his mind sorted, selected, codified, the information with which it had been fed. What he had to decide, the question that had remained unanswered was when to act? While the chief mover remained unidentified was it wise to act? But again was there really a 'chief mover', one man in absolute control? It seemed to Sir Jacob that he was probably dealing with a hydra. What he had to remember was that the money made from the sales went into the coffers of the terrorists and financed the purchase of bombs and small arms.

The office was in darkness now, only the lights outside the windows provided light in the room. Sir Jacob often would sit thus and Mavis knew that he was not to be disturbed, that he would emerge finally primed with decisions. It must have been over an hour and a half before he stood in the doorway of his room. 'Mavis,' he said, 'would you please make me some tea.'

'Certainly, Sir Jacob.'

Sir Jacob turned back into the room and switched on the desk lamp. He had decided to wait, to postpone action.

It was, however, within minutes of this that Nanny telephoned with the news of Rory's kidnapping: plans were once more uncertain.

CHAPTER TWELVE

Nairobi Interlude

'With my bow and arrow, I killed Cock Robin'

THE old road to Nairobi winds up the escarpment past the little chapel built by Italian prisoners of war when they had been working on the road's construction. The state of the road was awful, full of potholes and with broken, ragged edges. The road was usually thick with lorries and buses belching out thick, noisome fumes and, because grossly overloaded, crawling at a snail's pace. It was practically impossible to pass on the road up the escarpment and if one got stuck behind one of the lorries one's lungs were choked with the filthy smoke and fumes from the exhausts and one's eyes were stung by the acrid gases. This day I was unlucky and fretted with suppressed frustration, anxious to get to Nairobi, and eager to escape the smell and smoke.

There was no difficulty about Andrew's ticket, I paid with my American Express Card, then I made my way from the British Airways office to Oxbridge House, and then to the third floor. It seemed a small, unimportant suite of offices; in the outer office, the one I entered, besides the receptionist a plain-clothes man sat reading a paperback. I was expected and was ushered almost immediately into the office of Joab arap Kirui. He sat behind a plain wooden desk in a small room, the windows overlooked a car park, a rather faded large photograph of Mt Kenya was the only decoration. Noticeably missing were the portraits of the President and his predecessor. I wondered why.

NAIROBI INTERLUDE

'Come in,' he said. 'Come in and sit down.'

'Thank you, sir.' I shook his hand – a firm no-nonsense grip.

'Sit down, sit down.'

In front of him was a slim buff manila envelope and a pink folder.

'Now,' he said when I had settled, 'now what's all this about?'

'Sir Jacob,' I said, 'tells me that he has already spoken to you.'

'Yes, that's correct, he has; but what happened last night?' I told him the whole story, including the part about Andrew and the negatives.

'Hm, we have been watching that farm for some time now, the Major is not a pleasant person, but he has powerful friends in the Government, we have to be very sure before we act.'

'Sir?'

'Yes.'

'If you acted now, went to the farm, got him deported, he might be able to destroy much of the evidence.'

'That is true.'

'Sir, would it not be better, for the moment, just to observe and note?'

'It might well be, but I'm not too sure.'

'Yes, sir.'

'I think we have another lead, a visitor, a regular visitor from Pakistan, arrived yesterday, Major Hall met him and Mrs Moore was lunching with him today.'

'Do you know his name?'

'Yes, it is Gul Mohamed Khan, he's an exporter/importer according to our immigration records, he's involved in the fruit and vegetable business and also in the carpets that the dhows bring down from the Gulf and Baluchistan.'

'No drugs?'

'We don't know definitely, only suspect.'

'And Mrs Moore?'

'Probably no more than a go-between,' he grinned at the unintentional play on words, 'a messenger between the London end and here: but we have no proof. I certainly don't believe she is a principal.'

'What do you want me to do?'

He explained, 'We think that the principals are dissatisfied with Hall, he's made himself too conspicuous, he can't suppress his tendency to throw his weight about; we should not alert them any more – we must just watch. I think that you should play the innocent, cultivate

Mrs Moore – but for heaven's sake get your brother out of here as quickly as possible.'

'I intend to, sir, I have the ticket already.'

'Good, yes, that's very good. You know, we are pretty sure that we have pinpointed the route the drugs take out of Kenya.'

'Yes.'

'Twice a week for most of the year the Major sends vegetables to London and Paris by air – you've seen "Kenya Beans" in London West End greengrocers, even in July – the drugs go with the consignments. Mrs Moore, so Sir Jacob has discovered, is one of the directors of a Covent Garden wholesalers. The drugs go to her company and then are distributed throughout the country and to Europe through the lobster trade with France.'

It seemed so easy. Then I asked:

'How do the drugs get here, they aren't grown locally are they?'

'No, that's where Gul Mohamed Khan comes in. The drugs come to Mombasa or Lamu aboard the dhows – the old trade route – and from these by many different means to Nairobi, to one of the vegetable-packing stations.'

'Why don't you stop it now?'

'Well, the point is that Sir Jacob is not quite ready: his Department's concern, as you know, is not the drugs themselves but the fact that the money made from their sale is being used to finance terrorism – principally the IRA, this is the way the cash for arms is collected.'

'No, he hadn't told me; but it makes sense.' I remembered clearly the men in the hotel in Tiree. I had wondered then what they were really doing, now it was obvious. Captain Joab stood up.

'That's all for the moment, but we will keep a close watch on the Major, and please do not do anything foolish about your brother and tell him to play it cool, play it very cool.'

'I certainly will,' I said, 'and thank you for listening.'

'Not at all, it has been a pleasure, and', he added 'please keep in touch.'

When I left Captain Joab's office it was towards the end of the afternoon and Nairobi was beginning to go home – I had little inclination to get entangled in the traffic so I drove to the Norfolk for tea, to wait there for the rush to subside. I drank my tea and watched the world and the guests. My mind was buzzing with thoughts and questions that my interview with Captain Joab had engendered. One thing I was certain about was that the sooner we could get Andrew to London the better.

By the time I was ready to leave the worst of the traffic queues had dwindled, the jams cleared, and the maniac drivers were enfolded in the bosoms of their families. I had an uneventful run back to the farm – no smoke-belching buses or long-distance lorries impeded me. Dad had already returned and was clucking like an old hen. He had insisted on summoning Elsie and was catechizing her. He was standing before the fireplace, glass in hand, not quite sure whether he was the Grand Inquisitor or an angry outraged father.

'Dad, please, don't fuss, all is under control, really it is. I've booked a flight for Andrew – next Saturday – and I've spoken to my office and they'll look after him, he can stay at my flat for as long as he likes, or go up to Scotland. Nanny and Rory would love to see him.'

'That's all very well, but what I want to know is . . .'

'Dad,' I interrupted, 'I'll tell you later, I promise, but for now, please trust me and wait.'

'Damn it all, Adam, Andrew's my son and I'm entitled to know, why can't you tell me now?'

'No, Dad, no, please, wait.'

After some effort I managed to persuade my father to accept Andrew's explanation, even if only temporarily. Dr Elsie helped. I knew that he blamed my visit for what had happened, and in this he was of course right, or at least only partly right, for it was not my visit that had caused Major Hall to attempt Andrew's corruption. If my father had known of this he would have hit the roof and would have driven over to Hall's farm to horsewhip him. The explosion would have been memorable.

That night when the lights had gone out and the servants had retired to their quarters I went into my father's room – he was sitting in an armchair reading – and told him what had happened. I outlined the steps that Captain Joab was taking and explained the reasons behind them. My father had lacked patience and had grumbled at the advice that I had passed on to him.

'Do nothing' was not the kind of suggestion that commended itself to him. He also wanted to waken Andrew – he was furious with him, but I suspected that part of the fury was really anger with himself; he should have noticed, should have been aware of what was going on. My remonstrances that he could not possibly have known failed to convince him.

'Damn it all, Adam, this man must be stopped now – I owe it to my friends as well as to Andrew: their children need protection.'

'No, Father, no, let Joab's plan have a chance, please, he needs to collect evidence against the whole gang.'

In the end he compromised.

'I'll give you a week, if nothing happens by then I'll blow up.'

'All right, Dad, it's a deal.'

One of the dogs barked, then another – outside something was moving, probably a jackal or some cat, a genet perhaps. The night was full of noises, noises interwoven into a rich and varied background of sounds.

We went out on to the verandah, the dogs quietened when we spoke to them. The stars sparkled and glittered like sequins on velvet dress – a warm breeze soft as breath and heavy with the smells of the cooling earth ruffled the creepers that covered the roof. Peace returned.

'I'll make some tea, Adam, you wait here.'

My father shuffled off to the kitchen. I watched the night.

CHAPTER THIRTEEN

Rory in Danger

'Queensberry rules? Not bloody likely.'

THE men who control criminal empires are often mild of demeanour, though when their wealth or position are in jeopardy, they become ruthless, heartless and impervious to the demands either of friendship or of justice. Human life, not a rare resource, is expendable. In the card room of one of the clubs that grace Pall Mall four men were playing bridge. The club, with a solid early Victorian stone façade pitted by pollution, grimy, in need of a thorough scrubbing, stands four square. A declaration not only of stability but also, perhaps above else, of the supreme self-confidence that characterized Victorian Britain – a self-confidence not untouched by a certain amount of smugness. Clubs such as this epitomize what the political and social columnists of today call 'The Establishment'. Clubs patronized by those whom the contemporary equivalent of the man on the Clapham Omnibus would think of as 'them' as against his 'us'. In such a club, in its card room on the day on which I saw Captain Joab, the cards were cut and dealt. South was bidder, the score, love all.

    South a youngish middle-aged solicitor, a specialist in commercial law, regarded his hand. 'There is', he said, 'an unsatisfactory report from Nairobi, Hall seems to have bungled his end of the operation. *One Diamond.*'

    West had lately succeeded his father, a Labour peer, rootless,

	raffish, permanently broke, able and buyable. Bought. *'One Spade.'*
North	South's partner, one of those international businessmen of no identifiable nationality and holding at least one passport of convenience. *'Two Hearts.'*
East	An ex-police officer now running his own security firm, grey, formidable, taciturn. 'Shall we take Masson Out? *No Bid.'*
South	'Not yet, later. *Two no trumps.'*
West	'Is that wise do you think? *No Bid.'*
North	'But what about the woman? *Three no trumps.'*
East	'Surely some action is necessary now? *No Bid.'*
South	'Of course we have to move, it is plain what we must do. *No Bid.'*
West	*'No Bid.* It is not plain to me.'

South, who seemed to be the head of the group, waited for West to lead, North, dummy, put down his hand, then South spoke, looking directly at North. 'We must get the boy, he is their weakness.' North rose, he looked at South, 'I'll arrange it,' and went out of the card room. The game proceeded, the contract made, North returned. 'It is all arranged, we should know by this time tomorrow.'

A wintry smile flickered across South's face.

'Excellent.' He turned to West, 'your deal I believe.'

They were playing a game. David was trying, not it must be admitted with too much success, to cheer Rory up. The absence in Kenya of his uncle had begun to undermine the boy's confidence. He walked with head bowed, dejectedly, the usual bounce had gone; he dragged his feet.

'Geese?'

'A gaggle.'

'Red deer?'

'A herd.'

'Right. Goldfinches?'

'I know, we saw some on the teazles the other day; Uncle told me, a charm.'

'Yes, and cats?'

'Cats?'

'Um, yes, cats.'

There was a longish pause. Rory's brow wrinkled in concentration. 'A flock?' He made a guess.

'No; a flock of cats! Not a flock, nor indeed a herd nor a covey – think, Rory, think. Guess again.'

He guessed again. 'A stalk.' Then, 'No, no, David, I know, a pounce, it's a pounce of cats.'

'That's not bad, a pounce, but it's wrong; you could not have guessed. Actually, it's a clowder, a clowder of cats.'

Rory repeated the word. 'A clowder. "Clowder" is a nice word. What does it mean?'

'It's an old word, medieval, I think; it probably means a crowd or cluster.'

'Another, please.'

'Well,' David stopped and looked across the loch; above, rain clouds were gathering and a few seagulls circled, the surface of the loch was still, reflecting the clouds. 'I know, whales, yes, what is a collection of whales called?'

Rory thought. He and David were on their way to the Canon's house. It was the day for his Latin lesson. 'I know, I know, it's a shoal. I'm right, aren't I?'

'Well, well, shoal's not exactly wrong; it's all right to say shoal, but it's not the pukka word, the one used for example in *Moby Dick*, but you haven't yet read the story of the great white whale, or have you?'

'No, but I've seen the book on Uncle's shelves. He said "Wait for a year or two, it's pretty hard going".'

'I'll tell you the word. I think it's a good one, it is pod, a pod of whales.'

'I like it, I like it.' Rory danced down the path. 'A pod of whales.' He chanted, 'A pod, I've seen a pod of whales.'

The door opened, the Canon's wife stood in the doorway. 'Yes,' she said, 'and no doubt a nye of pheasants and a wisp of snipe to say nothing of a crash of rhinoceroses.'

'You know!'

'Yes, Rory, I'm a very old woman and during my long life a lot of the detritus of literature has been washed up on the shores of my knowledge.'

'This is David. He's a kind of cousin of Uncle's. He's here until Uncle comes back.' Dejection, temporarily banished, returned.

'How do you do?' She held out her hand.

'Very well, thank you.'

'Rory, you go along to the Canon, he's in the study waiting for you. I'll take David into the kitchen and we'll have a cup of tea and a talk; come along.'

Rory tapped on the study door, dark stained with a porcelain knob.

'Come in. Hello, Rory, how are you?'

'All right, Father.' He sat down and took out his Latin primer.

The Canon looked across the study table at the boy sitting opposite him. Instead of the usual volcano bubbling with talk and questions, there was a sad, quiet, withdrawn child.

'Rory, what's the matter?'

'Nothing, Father.' Then, 'Father?'

'Yes?'

'Father, where is heaven?'

'Where is heaven?' The Canon repeated the question, half to himself. 'Where is heaven? I can tell you where it isn't. It is not up there, beyond the stars, it is not to be found in some far away galaxy waiting to be discovered by Captain Kirk or the Astronomer Royal.' He paused. 'Nor, of course, is hell down there under our feet. But I can't truthfully answer your question, Rory, except to admit straight away that I don't know. Why do you ask?'

'Where are Mum and Dad and Penelope, what's happened to them?' There was in the voice an underlying panic.

The old man thought for some moments.

'Rory, when someone dies, they are, as you know, usually buried or cremated, and their bodies or their ashes go back to the earth. You've seen how a dead insect gradually turns to dust, crumbles away, or how the body of a dead mouse or bird disintegrates, helped quite often by ants and beetles. Well, our bodies do the same, they become part of the earth, they nourish plants or insects, they enrich the soil; in modern terms, you could say that they are recycled. What happens to a body is not a mystery. There is no real problem, we can see what happens. Your body after all was just a place in which you lived. Does that make sense?'

'Yes,' a rather hesitant yes, 'yes, Father.'

'Now, Rory, think, think about yourself, about you, look at yourself. Your father and mother made you, without them there would have been no you, they live, their lives continue in you, just as your grandparents lived in them – in you live all those past generations of your family, just as in your children, if you have any, will you and your parents and grandparents live. People often say that "you have the eyes of your father" or "the family nose".' He paused, his mind travelling back to the death of his daughter, a shadow of grief touched his expression as he remembered the grave in Africa. 'You know, when Cressida died I felt then as though a part of me had died too; in a way I suppose it had, for we had no other children, but in another way she still lives, not only in my head, in my mind, but that what she did, what she was, still lives, still goes on. I remember what she said and what she did, and what she loved influences what I do and what I think. But when I see Cressida again, she won't be a little girl pale and dying, and I won't be a decrepit old man, toothless, lame, muddled. Death does not freeze us. I don't know what she or I will be, but I'm sure that we will need no introduction. Think of yourself; your father was a doctor, he saved many lives, he healed and treated the sick, in all those patients whom he helped he still lives; perhaps, too, he sometimes got angry and frustrated and shouted at a servant or a nurse, perhaps he wrote an unkind letter to a friend or colleague – those actions may have had a bad effect, and that effect, alas, lives on, just as the effect of his goodness lives on too; nothing really dies, what happens is that everything changes, we do, all the time, and the changes are influenced by many factors. "The acorn becomes the oak tree." '

'Yes, Father, I think I understand, but where are Mum and Dad now?'

'I don't know, that's the truth, Rory, I simply don't know, but I can tell you what I believe. I know, as you do, that out there is the loch, that in my garden are the bees in their hives, and the cabbages and Sweet Williams. I know that you have a dog called Cracker. Those things I know, I can see and touch them. Other things, other facts I accept: that Julius Caesar landed in Britain in 55 BC, that Leonardo da Vinci painted the 'Last Supper'. I can't prove them, I have to rely on all sorts of different evidence, written and archaeological. I have to trust what other people have said or written. But there is one thing, and this is important, this is the core of the matter, if you believe, as I do, in Jesus Christ, that He is really the Son of God, if you have faith in Him, then when He talks about heaven or paradise you believe Him although you can't ask Him face to face, but you don't know in the same way that you know the loch is there. When Jesus said to the penitent thief at the Crucifixion, "This day shalt thou be with me in Paradise," He was not lying, but He never said where paradise was. The Gospels are full of parables, remember in St Matthew how Jesus says: "Suffer little children, and forbid them not, to come unto me; for of such is the kingdom of heaven." Rory, the crux of the matter is, must be, belief in Jesus. Heaven is a gigantic mystery which one will only solve when one goes there. I can't answer your question. I'm very sorry. I can't tell you where you father and mother are. I don't know.'

Rory stretched out his hand and placed it on the hand of the old priest as it lay on the table, the small brown one none too clean but pulsing with life lay for a moment on top of the thin, translucent, blue-veined skeletal hand of the Canon.

'Father, I think I understand, it's a mystery, no one really dies, not all of them.'

'I think so, Rory, I do think so.'

'But it's Uncle. Why did he have to go to Kenya?'

Ah, so that is the real problem, that is why the other question had been asked, that is why the boy looks so dejected. The Canon pondered the question. Rory was feeling lost, betrayed, rejected. He was frightened that once again he would be left alone, bereft of love and security. 'Rory, he had to go, it was a matter of duty, he did not want to leave you. You know that, don't you?'

'Yes, Father, but . . .' His eyes began to fill with tears.

'Rory, remember, there is this strange awkward thing called duty. It is, can often be, horrible for those affected by it, but there come times when one knows instinctively that one has to do something that one may not want to do; one knows that it will hurt and distress those one loves, but it is something compelling, one just has to do it. Your uncle's not deserting you. Indeed, one of the reasons that he has gone is because he feels that he has to – for you. He mustn't let you down. In the past he only had himself to think about, now he has you, you've changed his outlook, now he has to listen.' And, remember, you are not alone, you have Nanny, and us. We're here, you know that, you have Sandy, and don't forget you have Cracker, and now you have David. Now come on, open that primer. We must do some work – second declension nouns today.'

Not long after, the Canon's wife came in, a glass of milk and a slice of cake for Rory, a glass of sherry for the Canon.

'Time to finish, dear; you all right, Rory?'

'Yes, thank you.'

'Good. Well don't be too long. David's waiting for you.'

RORY IN DANGER

Rory drank his milk. The lesson was over. He packed his books away and was dismissed with a canonical blessing. 'Rory, remember one thing. It is important. You are not alone, remember.'

'Yes, Father, thank you.' He made his way to the kitchen. Here David and Mrs Buchanan were immersed in discussion of some recipe as obscure as it was probably delicious.

'Come in, Rory, have another piece of cake.'

'Thank you.'

'David and I have been having a splendid time. He says, but I'm not sure I believe him, that he is a good cook.'

'He makes good sausages and mash, but Nanny does most of the cooking. She says he's just an amateur.'

'Rory, that's not fair. Traitor.'

'It's true.'

'You ruffian. I'll remember that. Come on, we had better be off. Thank you for the tea and cake.'

'You're always welcome here, remember that, and look after Rory, we've grown very fond of him.' Rory glowed.

Rory and David started back, a soft drizzle had begun to fall.

'What do you want to do, Rory, do you want to go fishing?'

'Yes, let's go fishing.'

'Come on then, we'll get the rods and Cracker. He'll need a walk.'

A van drew up, unwashed, battered, unmemorable.

'Want a lift?'

'No, thank you.'

'I think you do.' He had a gun. The rear door of the van opened and the second man got out.

'Come here.' This to Rory.

'No.' Fear gripped him, he stood shaking. 'No.'

'Don't be stupid.' The second man grabbed him, throwing a greasy rug over his head. David threw himself forward, the first man shot him. Three faint plops, there was a silencer.

'We'll dump him by the loch.'

David was bundled into the van; it started, after a few minutes it stopped. The door opened and David was dumped behind some bushes, unconscious and bleeding. The van backed, turned and within a few minutes was on its way to Glasgow. The first part of the plan was accomplished.

A prick in the arm and Rory was out. The van stopped. 'Come

on, get him out.' Still with the rug over his head, Rory was transferred to a car.

'On the floor,' covered, although night had fallen. The car began the second part of the journey to Glasgow. It stopped outside a tower block in one of the grey, depressing Glasgow suburbs. The street was empty, a cat slipped quickly away under the remnants of a fence. The boy was carried into the building. For once the lift was working, cleaned, the scatological and impossible biological directives painted over. The entrance to the flat was cold, impersonal, but spotlessly clean. Rory was thrown on to a bed, his hands and feet bound. He was still insensible from the drug.

'What's next?'

'We'll be told. Get some food, I'm hungry.'

Donald, one of the railway porters from the local station, leant his bicycle against the rowan tree and walked down towards the loch, Beauty, his black labrador bitch, with him. The earlier rain had stopped. The afternoon sun, low in the sky, was reflected by the water, dazzling like shining scales of a salmon. Although late in the year, a few midges danced above the tracks. As he neared the loch, he heard a low moaning – he looked at Beauty, she had stiffened, become alert, suspicious. 'Go girl.' he ordered and she, sniffing the ground, moved towards a clump of evergreen bushes into which she then disappeared. Then she began barking, but not an aggressive or a frightened bark, but one of those demanding, imperious calls. Donald ran forward and there lying on the ground was a young man – David – he opened his eyes. 'They've got Rory, I'm shot,' then he passed out.

He had been found just in time, exposure and loss of blood would, in half an hour or so, have proved fatal. Nanny, shocked and tearful, nevertheless kept her nerve. She rang the emergency number on the telephone pad, Sir Jacob's number.

'Yes? *Associated Fruits.*'

'I must speak to Sir Jacob, it's very urgent.'

'Who is that please.'

'Nanny Masson, Rory's nanny, please hurry.'

A new voice.

'Hullo, can I help you?'

'Yes, please, I must speak with Sir Jacob.'

'I am sorry he is at a meeting, I cannot disturb him, will you leave a message and a number so that he can ring you back?'

'Young woman, get him now, stop havering, tell him I will speak to him, tell him Rory's been kidnapped and David shot.'

Silence, a click, then within half a minute, 'Jacob Menzies here.'

Nanny told her story – Sir Jacob listened.

'Thank you, Nanny,' he said, 'we'll take charge, don't worry too much, we'll get Rory back.'

'Don't be silly, of course I'll worry, I was left in charge.'

'I'm sorry, Nanny, that was silly, I know you'll worry, but please trust us.'

'And my Adam, who'll tell him?'

'We'll get in touch with him. I'll speak to him myself, and, Nanny?'

'Yes, sir?'

'Nanny, don't go too far away from the telephone or the house, they may try to get in touch with you. Our man will soon be with you but it will be you they will get in touch with, at least at first.'

'Very good, sir.'

'And, Nanny, don't despair, please.'

'I'll do my best.'

The Department moved. Within a very short time one of Sir Jacob's most senior lieutenants was in an Army helicopter on his way North. The Home Office is not unlike one of those early wireless sets it takes a little time to warm up.

In the hospital the surgeon extracted three bullets from David, two from his shoulder and one from the broken leg. Too exhausted, too drugged to be questioned, he slept, a troubled unrestful sleep, sweat dampening his forehead and upper arms. Fever – the doctors feared that pneumonia might set in.

Poor Nanny fretted, nothing could calm her agitation; illogically she blamed herself, she should have kept a more observant eye on Rory; a uniformed constable was at the house just as there was one at the hospital outside David's ward, flirting with the younger nurses.

Rory was kept in the Glasgow apartment for three nights. Then, late, he was drugged again and put on the floor of a car, wrapped in the same greasy rug. The car then drove back to the outskirts of the village. There, standing by one of the tracks through the forest, waited the forester.

'Yes,' he answered, the area had been thoroughly searched, police, army, locals, nothing had been discovered. The part-ruined and deserted cottage high above the line of firs had been used temporarily as a search-post, now it was deserted. Normalcy had returned, at least on the surface. The driver listened, nodded, money passed.

'I'll be back tomorrow sometime. Quick, take the boy.'

'Right.' He threw the boy over his shoulder and set out into the hills to the ruin, followed by the second man. The car sped on to Oban, stopping only at a call box at Connell Ferry.

'Second stage of the mission accomplished.'

'Good. Get back here as soon as you can. Leave the rest to us.'

Far away in the hut, Rory began to awaken.

CHAPTER FOURTEEN

Alarms and Excursions

'Tarry not. I beg you, Madam, for the wings of time are tipped with the feathers of death'

My father and I were sitting on the verandah enjoying the peace and quietness of that time when day elides with night, albeit in the tropics this is a brief period, for unlike the temperate areas where dusk and dawn linger and gently fade, in the tropics and on the equator the sun disappears almost but not quite as quickly as an electric light bulb darkens when the switch is turned off. A decanter of whisky and a bowl of ice stood on the table between us, fingers of light scratched the belly of the sky and in the distance a jackal howled and shortly was answered, versicle and response, a lovers' duet. Inside the house the telephone rang. Ali appeared.

'*Bwana*,' he said to me, 'a call from London.'

'That must be Sir Jacob,' I said, and went in with the whisky glass in my hand.

'Hullo, Adam Masson here.'

'Adam, this is Jacob Menzies.' Then, there was a pause. 'Adam, I've some bad news for you.'

I felt fear creep up my stomach. 'Yes?'

'They've got Rory, kidnapped him.'

This is what I had always feared, a hidden fear unaired in the day but in the night a cause of sleeplessness.

'Rory?'

'Yes, this is what happened.' Sir Jacob outlined the events of the kidnapping and of David's wounding.

'I must come back.'

'No, no, no, stay where you are, we will do all we can: the boy will be all right.'

'How the devil do you know?'

'They will want to use him as a bargaining factor, so they will look after him.'

Not, I thought, very convincing.

'What do they want? Who are they?'

'They have not been in touch yet, we're waiting. They may want to confuse us by not getting in touch.'

'And Nanny?'

'She is anxious, very upset, we're looking after her, there's a constable at the house.'

'What shall I do?'

'Nothing for the moment, we'll keep in touch, please believe me we won't give up, he'll soon be back – Good night.'

'Good night.' I put the receiver back on its hook.

Rory, they had Rory, my mind filled and emptied, memories, images, worries. I stood silent.

'Adam, Adam, what is it?' My father stood in doorway looking in from the verandah. I pushed him aside, without really seeing him, and leant on the balustrade gazing out at the sky, studded with stars. How long I stood there I don't know, but later my father said that I had stayed there for at least ten minutes before I turned round.

'Dad, they have Rory, he's gone.'

'Good God!' then, 'Sit down. Here, have a drink.'

I had one drink then another. I did not want to speak and my father was sensitive enough to recognize this.

After some time he spoke.

'Adam, I think you should go to bed, we can't do anything now, but we will ring in the morning and then if it is necessary get you on the plane back to England – that shouldn't be too difficult.'

My father got up from his chair and for a moment stood by mine. He touched my shoulder, it was comforting to know that he was there, someone I could trust.

'Thanks, Dad.' He said nothing.

'Dad, I'm going to Elsie's to ring Joab.'

'Yes, that's a good idea.'

When I got through to Joab, he was in his office. I found that Sir Jacob had already telephoned.

'Right,' Joab said, 'we've decided to advance our operations. The Major and Mrs Moore are at Muthaiga tonight – so we'll pick them up in the early hours.'

'I'll ring you in the morning.'

'Yes, do that, but now you go to bed – forget this conversation. Good night.'

'Good night.'

'Oh, one thing Masson, trust Sir Jacob, he is very good, I know.'

I put down the receiver and returned to my father.

'Dad?'

'Yes, Adam.'

'I think I'll sit here for a little, you go to bed.'

'Very well, but don't stay up too late.'

'I won't, I promise.'

'And, Adam, don't fret, nothing has ever been accomplished by fretting. It should be all right, I'm sure it will.'

Sure, certain, how could anyone know, really know? Platitudes and pious hopes poured on the problem like oil on wounds, were not a cure but at least a palliative. After an hour I got up and staggered to my room, my mind befuddled with whisky, my limbs heavy with despair. In my room I lay on my bed and wept.

When I stumbled out to breakfast the next morning, my head on fire and my stomach churning, Captain Joab was seated on the verandah drinking coffee with my father and Andrew; outside two police vehicles were parked in the drive and a helicopter stood in the paddock beyond.

'Hullo.'

'I have some good news for you, Mr Masson, I've told your father.'

'Yes?'

'This morning very early we arrested Hall and Mrs Moore, they're being held in Nairobi. I have deportation orders.'

'Andrew?'

'Yes, at the same time we went to the farm with a search warrant and we found the negatives, a number of young people round here seem to have fallen victim to the good Major's actions; but so far no drugs have been found. Here,' he threw an envelope on to the table, 'here are the photographs.' My father put out a hand. 'No.' I picked the envelope up, 'I'll destroy these now.' I took them over to the fireplace and, striking a match, set the package on fire.

'That's very sensible, Mr Masson.'

'What about the others, what are you going to do with them?'

'We'll destroy them — eventually, but we need to identify all the subjects, they may be able to help us.'

'And the Major?'

'Although we have not found any drugs yet — my men are still searching — we have found some very interesting files. There seems to be a definite connection with the Pakistani and with a firm in London. And,' he hesitated before going on, 'and Sir Jacob is sending two of his experts out to help us. I asked for them,' he smiled, 'Sir Jacob is very persuasive.'

CHAPTER FIFTEEN

Rory, a Hostage

'The woods are lovely, dark and deep.'

RORY, his feet tied together and his hands stretched behind his back and bound with tape, was in a near-derelict cottage high in the hills above a glen, now heavily forested, through which no public road ran, only an old track and the makeshift roads made by the Forestry Commission years ago when they began planting.

Who were his captors? There were three, one a young man, intolerant, an adherent of one of the far left revolutionary groups convinced of the wickedness of the 'system'. Another darker, quieter of demeanour, a citizen of one of the Eastern Mediterranean countries, not an ideologist but a mercenary, well paid. The third, one of the foresters, a local man.

Rory was scared and wanted to relieve himself.

'Please,' he said. 'Please.'

'What is it?'

'I want to spend a penny.'

The young man untied his feet and lifted the boy from the chair, then untied his hands.

'No funny business, right?' He led him outside the cottage, the trees grew close to it, although on one side whether by intent or accident there was a small patch of bare land on which there were neither trees nor bushes.

Darkness was falling.

The mist that had formed as night fell and the trees round the cottage blocked out any light – but the forester covered the windows with old sacking. 'I'll light a fire, it will not be seen; we are too far away.' There was plenty of dead wood and soon a fire was crackling on the hearth. There was no hot food but his captors made tea, hot, sweet and milky, and there was bread and cheese. While he ate they had his hands untied but not his feet. As soon as he had finished they tied him up.

'I'm sorry that we have to do this, but if we sleep or have to leave you we cannot risk your escaping.' They threw a couple of blankets over him and, tired and mentally as well as physically exhausted, he soon fell asleep.

'I shall have to go now,' said the forester, 'it will not be good for me to be away too long.'

'I'll come with you, I need to telephone.' The young man with the creaky accent got up. 'You'll be all right here, Ahmed, I won't be too long.'

They disappeared into the night. Ahmed threw more wood on the fire, turned out the hurricane lamp and lay down to sleep.

When I woke I had felt as though my head was full of little men with hammers trying to break out. My mouth was dry, my eyes stinging, bloodshot and puffed up – I looked as I felt. Joab and his men had gone, he back to Nairobi by the helicopter, the cars to Hall's farm where the centre of operations had been established. I drank some black coffee. The telephone rang. My father answered it. 'It's London.'

I took the 'phone.

'Adam Masson here.'

'Hold on please, sir, Sir Jacob would like to speak to you.'

'Adam!'

'Have you found Rory, is he safe?'

'No, not yet, but it should not be long, my best men are there.'

Words so trite, so passionless, poured out in a spate, unstoppable, like a swollen stream after a cloudburst. The upshot of this conversation was that I discovered firstly that Rory was still missing and secondly that so far no message had been received and no demands made.

There had been silence.

'I'm coming home.'

'No, no, no, stay where you are, you're more use to us, and to Rory, in Kenya.'

'But I must come. Rory . . .'

'No, Adam, no, just listen. You really must trust us, if you come back there would be nothing more that you could do – you're far too "noticeable". They would recognize you straight away and could use you – it would not help Rory at all, not at all.'

After many protests I allowed myself to be persuaded not to return to England immediately, but to stay where I was. Sir Jacob told me that it had now been confirmed that the drugs were coming to Britain in consignments of beans, avocados and courgettes from Kenya and that from the wholesalers they were distributed throughout the country and beyond, coming to Tiree by fishing boats and from there sent to the continent through the export of live lobsters. It seemed an unlikely and unnecessary exercise but it had worked successfully for a number of years.

The day after Rory's abduction, in the early afternoon, the doctor's son Alexander – Sandy – Rory's particular friend, went with his father to see Nanny. An idea had formed in his mind but he kept it secret, lest it were sat on by Authority and forbidden. Poor Nanny looked tired and depressed despite her efforts to be calm, cheerful and optimistic. Her thoughts were not only with Rory but with Adam.

'I wish, doctor, that he were here.'

'I know, Nanny, but it seems he can't be.'

'Nanny, would you like me to take Cracker for a walk?'

'Well, Sandy, that would be kind, thank you, he does need some exercise.'

'I think I'll go and see the Canon.'

The loch was coated with mist, so dense that the farther shore had disappeared. The soft drizzle was turning to rain, it was a thoroughly depressing winter's afternoon, a time for log fires and television, not for searches for a lost small boy.

Sandy, after his talk with Canon Buchanan, had made up his mind. The Canon had listened and had then distinguished the dangers of certain courses: 'You are young, Sandy,' he said, 'and you should not lightly attempt any action that would or could cause worry to your parents and friends.'

'Yes, Father.'

The old man smiled and sat without speaking.

'Father?'
'Yes, Sandy?'
'Father, do you trust Cracker?'
'He is a fine dog.'
'Would he let me down?'
'No, certainly not intentionally, it would be out of his character to do so.'
'Thank you, Father, I'll have to go now.'
'One moment, Sandy.' The boy stood quietly by the door, looking back at the old man by the blazing fire. 'Sandy, remember always one thing, put neither yourself nor your feelings first, do you understand?'
'Yes, Father.'
'Good, then go with God.'

Sandy shut the door quietly behind him, shutting out the warmth and security of certainty.

Inside the room the old man sat looking into the fire. Here his wife found him: the flames had long since died, only a faint red glow remained. She shivered, saying nothing but putting small kindling and logs on the ashes.

'I'll bring tea in a few minutes, darling.'

By the time that she returned the logs were burning, flames leaping up the chimney and the old man had returned from his journey.

'I'm old and rather foolish, I no longer have a clear vision.'
'Yes, darling.'
'To every season there is a time to cast away stories, and a time to gather stories together.'
'Is there any news?'
'No, but there are more police than ever, they seem confident.'

Sandy stood at the Canon's gate, Cracker waited expectantly at his side. He made up his mind.

'C'm'on Cracker.' The two set out down to the river and across the bridge. They struck out towards the conifer plantations. When they reached the edge where the foresters' tracks emerged Sandy stopped.

'Now look, Cracker, we've got to find Rory, but only you can, do you understand? We must find Rory!' He knelt in front of the dog and spoke to him quietly and intensely, explaining to him what he wanted done. The dog listened and when Sandy had finished licked his hand and growled softly.

'Find him, find Rory, please, Cracker, please!'

It was a strangely pathetic sight, the boy talking earnestly to the dog, oblivious to his surroundings.

They walked along the edge of the plantation; two figures, the forester and a younger man, came from the trees towards them.

'Hullo.' The dog growled, the hair on its neck rising. 'Ssh, quiet, it's all right.'

The forester stopped: 'Any news of the boy?'

'No, the police think, so my father says, that Rory is by now in Glasgow.'

'That's likely, big place Glasgow.' He passed on. The dog throughout the conversation had been softly growling. When the forester had disappeared Sandy let go the collar.

'Now, Cracker, find Rory.'

The dog turned and began to follow the forester and his companion.

'No, no, not that way – we've got to find Rory.'

Cracker looked at Sandy. It seemed almost as though he were making an intelligent assessment of the situation to determine his course of action.

He sniffed round for a few moments, cocked his leg against a large stone, then with a quick backward glance at Sandy set off into the plantation, following the track down which the forester had lately come. He seemed in no doubt about which way to go. He trotted forward sniffing at intervals and pausing to look back to see whether Sandy was following.

Sandy felt uneasy and a little frightened, for within a couple of hours it would be dark and he had neither torch nor matches, but Cracker seemed so sure, so confident and he remembered the Canon's advice and he decided not to turn back; they had branched off the main path and were on a side track, overgrown and unused. Then, when more than half an hour had passed, and they were still climbing, the track suddenly emerged into a small clearing and there in front was a partly ruined cottage, a gleam of light in one window. Sandy held Cracker's collar.

'Ssh, Cracker, no barking.'

He stepped back into the trees and thought about what he should do. There was nothing to show that Rory was in the cottage, but the excitement of the dog and his own instinct made him feel sure that they had found him. Under cover of the trees he circled the clearing until he reached the other side of the cottage. Holding Cracker tightly by the collar he crept from the shelter of the trees to the cottage wall, edging himself round until he could look into the room. There he saw Rory, tied up and with him the saturnine man, who was smoking and looking at a newspaper.

The sensible thing would be for him to go back to the village and tell the authorities, but often in a crisis sense flies out of the window. What should he do? He withdrew and crouched hidden in the undergrowth. Then the decision was made for him. Cracker broke from his grasp and rushed barking into the cottage. Sandy flattened himself on the ground and held his breath. Inside the cottage Cracker raced to Rory and began licking his face, nuzzling him, friendship renewed, loyalty asserted. Rory cried with pleasure, 'Oh, Cracker, dear Cracker, how pleased I am to see you!'

The man, who had risen hurriedly to his feet and had run outside to check, came back into the room, a revolver in his hand.

'He must go.'

'No, no, please, please let him stay.'

Cracker growled, his teeth bared.

The man pondered. Certainly he thought the dog would keep the boy happy if it stayed; if he threw it out it might go back and bring the police. He was unwilling to shoot it because his gun had no silencer and the noise might be heard. There might possibly be people about.

'OK he can stay, but no funny business, that understood?'

'Oh thank you.' Tears were running down Rory's cheeks, he could not hold Cracker because his hands were tied but he could rest his head on the dog's wet side.

'Look now, I'm going to heat up some soup,' he checked Rory's bonds, they were tight enough. 'I'm sorry about this but orders must be obeyed.' He left the room firstly to go outside and collect some more wood and then into the back room where the food was kept and a primus stove had that day been installed.

Sandy emerged from the shadows and slipped into the cottage. He ran to Rory, and knelt beside him. 'Shhh – don't say a word, except to Cracker.' He took out his knife, cut the rope at the ankles then at the wrists.

'Come on,' he whispered. 'We must get away quickly.'

They slipped out into the plantation – dusk had fallen and a mist was settling in the glen and edging up the hillside obliterating the trees and the sharp edges of the rocks and forest limits.

'We'll get lost,' said Rory. 'What shall we do?'

'Cracker will lead us – don't worry.'

'Oh, Sandy, it is good to see you; I've been awfully scared.'

'It'll be all right, really, we'll get Cracker to lead us down.'

He took a piece of string from his pocket, but it was no good, it broke as he tied it to Cracker's collar.

'I know, my belt'll do, and yours,' said Sandy. They joined the belts and fixed them to the dog's collar.

'Now, Cracker, now take us home, please,' Rory whispered, rubbing his face in Cracker's coat.

'Hey, where are you?' The man came to the doorway shouting obscenities, he shone a powerful torch and searched the edge of the clearing, under the trees – nothing could be seen, and there was neither whisper nor sound of movement. He wondered what he should do. If he tried to find his way down the mountain without the forester he would surely get lost, if he showed too much light someone else might be alerted. So he decided for the moment to wait his comrade's return. He cursed and went back into the cottage.

Rory holding Cracker, and Sandy holding Rory, the boys and the dog made their way down the mountainside, stumbling, stubbing their toes on stones, stumps and fallen trees, their legs and hands torn by brambles, their faces scratched by low branches. They were cold and wet and very frightened, only Cracker seemed to know where they were going. It seemed to them like hours but in fact they had been walking for under an hour when they emerged on to a road.

They were undecided which way to go.

'Let's wait a minute, Rory.'

'All right.'

They sat down, two cold, wet, bedraggled, small boys and a panting dog, huddled together, frightened.

'Listen, Rory, listen, I hear a car, at least I think it is a car.'

'C'm'on we'll stop it.' In the distance, lights appeared, growing ever brighter. Oblivious to the danger that it might be the enemy, they stood at the road's edge gesticulating wildly, Cracker barking. The headlights illuminated them and the car slowed down and stopped. It was a police car, one of those sent to the area on Sir Jacob's instruction. A giant of a man got out. Rory ran to him. He stood looking up, strands of wet matted hair plastering his forehead, his face and hands scratched, his jeans and jersey mud-soaked, his body shaking with cold and exhaustion.

'I'm Rory, please take us home,' and he burst into tears; in a moment the giant had picked him up and was comforting him.

'It's all right, Rory, you're safe now, we'll take you home.' To Sandy, less exhausted, he held out a comforting hand. 'Good lad, now you and the dog get in the back.'

The car turned round and drove back to the village. Rory composed himself and by the time the car drew up in front of the cottage he was calmer, the panic had subsided.

'We'll 'phone your father,' the policeman said to Sandy.

'No, look, Rory, Dad's car is there.' So it was. The doctor had, when Sandy's absence was discovered, returned to the cottage. Nanny and the police sergeant had tried to pacify him. 'I'll skin him alive.'

Now, appraised by the car radio that the boys had been found, a reception committee was waiting.

They fussed like old hens, clucking with disapproval and concern at the scratches and cuts, the rope burns on Rory's ankles. It was, the boys thought, when they later compared notes, absolutely marvellous. Soon they were sitting in the kitchen, wrapped in blankets, bowls of hot soup in front of them and thickly-buttered slices of bread. It was hard for the doctor to conceal his pride in Sandy's resourcefulness and Sandy revelled in his approbation and in the safety of his presence.

The plain-clothes man, Sir Jacob's representative, asked a few questions but then said: 'The rest of the questions can wait until tomorrow. I think that these young men should be in bed.' He turned to Nanny and the doctor. 'We'll put a guard on all night so you won't need to worry.'

Sandy looked at his father. 'Dad, can I say here tonight, please?'

'Yes, I think that's a good idea, off you go – and Sandy.'

'Yes, Dad?'

'Well done; come here, I'm very very proud of you.'

'Dad, I was scared but I did have Cracker.'

The boys went off to bed.

'I'll be up in a minute,' said Nanny, 'so get into bed quickly.'

When they had gone Nanny turned to the policeman.

'What about Mr Masson, should I ring him with the news?'

'No, Nanny, Sir Jacob said that he would do that.'

Sir Jacob paced up and down his office, consumed with impatience, frustrated – all the international lines to Kenya were temporarily out of order or engaged, there was something wrong at the Kenya end, caused it was said by a tropical storm and the ensuing flood. He went to the television set that stood in the corner of his room and turned it on – BBC 2 – there was a war programme, an incursion into nostalgia. Songs of the First World War 'It's a long, long, trail a-winding,' the thin scratchy voice of a long-dead singer.

He switched to 1, football; to ITV, snooker; to Channel 4, an appalling serial. He switched off and resumed his pacing. His intercom buzzed.

'Yes, yes Mavis come in, come in.'

Mavis entered exuding competence (and smugness).

'Well?'

'Sir Jacob, some coffee?'

'No.'

'Sir Jacob, perhaps I should send a wire to the High Commissioner.'

'Yes, yes we could do that, but we have to be careful, I'll draft it now,' and after a pause, 'a good idea, Mavis, thank you, should've thought of it myself.'

'*Bwana*, the telephone.'

'Who is it?'

'*Bwana Mkubwa*, the High Commissioner.' I ran to the 'phone.

'Hullo, Masson here.'

'Good, now listen, I have some very good news for you.'

When I returned to the verandah tears were streaming down my face.

'Dad, Dad,' I struggled to speak 'Dad he's safe, Rory's been rescued.'

EPILOGUE

I
Et Ego in Arcadia

'True, I talk of dreams,
Which are the children of an idle brain,
Begot of nothing but vain fantasy;
Which is as thin of substance as the air.'

I HARDLY remembered what happened during the next few hours, but I do remember the immense relief and consuming tiredness. My father packed me off to bed, full of his best Malt and I slept for ten hours, only waking late the next morning. Then all was action. More instructions had come – I could return home. I booked for the following day. There was a great deal to clear up. Joab came to the farm and told us that the Major was being deported, he had chosen to go to South America, but Mrs Moore was released and asked to leave the country as soon as possible. She returned to collect her clothes, then she was off on her travels, to South Africa.

Gul Mohamed Khan was being sent back to Pakistan and his embassy had been informed and the small local men were already in prison, accused of trafficking in drugs.

EPILOGUE

II
Plus ça Change

'The lonely man will keep his loneliness
Will lie awake, will read, will write long letters
Will wander to and fro under the trees
Restlessly, while the leaves run from the wind.'

PINE logs spluttered and hissed in the grate and the air was perfumed with the sweet pungent smell of resin. Rory lay on the rug reading, Cracker at his feet, and I was comfortably sunk in an old comfortable armchair, a tumbler of whisky on the table by me, the *Times* crossword on my lap. It was very peaceful. Sparks leapt up the chimney. Nanny had gone home, albeit reluctantly – since the kidnapping she had persuaded herself that she stood between Rory, me, and disaster, and it was useless to suggest otherwise. In her eyes not only had I deserted my post in the middle of the action, but I had also evaded my duty. I had been enjoying myself while Rory was missing. Rory rolled over on to his back and lay like a dog or cat wanting its stomach tickled.'

'Uncle?'

'Yes, Rory?'

'This is good, isn't it?'

'Yes, it certainly is.'

'Uncle,' he stretched out his hand and held my ankle. 'Uncle, I do understand: I don't blame you.' He stopped, silence entered the room. 'It was awful.'

'I know,' I said, 'it was for me too, but we survived.' I rubbed his belly with my foot.

He stretched, ecstatically, and turned over.

'I'm hungry, is it nearly supper time?'

'Good?'

'Yes, almost perfect.'

It was a little like a *bombe flambé*, on fire outside, inside cool as air conditioning could ensure.

'Did you miss me?'

'Of course, and you?'

'Haven't I just proved it?'

Petros traced the vivid scar on Michael's side.

'Does it hurt?'

'No, not now.'

'Mikael.'

'Yes?'

Sir Jacob had called Michael to his office when he had left hospital and had thanked him for what he had done.

'We could use someone like you again,' he had said. 'If you grow bored let me know.'

Michael had smiled. He had, he felt, had more than enough excitement and danger for several lifetimes.

'Yes Sir, I will.'

Now he was back at work in the Gulf, reunited with Petros, relaxed and peaceful.

'Mikael.'

'Yes?'

'Mikael, I am betrothed, my family have found me a wife, I go back to Cyprus next month.'

The moment he had feared but which he had known to be inevitable had arrived.

'I shall return: it need not change.'

He stroked the head resting on his breast.

'Don't be silly, of course it will change, it must; but not yet.'

'That is right, we have a few weeks.'

Next day Michael made a reversed person to person telephone call to London. A somewhat irate Sir Jacob answered.

'Yes?'

'Hullo Sir Jacob, Michael McNab here, I have decided to accept your offer.'